SANTA FE WAGON BOSS

Alex Briscoe, the owner of a freighting firm, was making his way with his wagon train from Hays City to Santa Fe when plunderers struck and killed his men, stole his bullion and led away his horses. But Briscoe had seen the brand on one of their horses so he knew who to hunt down in his search for vengeance.

Cliff Farrell was born in Zanesville, Ohio, where earlier Zane Grey had been born. Following graduation from high school, Farrell became a newspaper reporter. Over the next decade he worked his way west by means of a string of newspaper jobs and for thirty-one years was employed, mostly as sports editor, for the *Los Angeles Examiner*. He would later claim that he began writing for pulp magazines because he grew bored with journalism. His first Western stories were written for *Cowboy Stories* in 1926 and his byline was A. Clifford Farrell. By 1928 this byline was abbreviated to Cliff Farrell, and this it remained for the rest of his career. In 1933 Farrell was invited to contribute a story for the first issue of *Dime Western*. He soon became a regular contributor to this magazine and to *Star Western* as well. In fact, many months he would have a short novel in both magazines. Farrell became such a staple at Popular Publications that by the end of the 1930s he was contributing as much as 400,000 words a year to their various Western magazines. In all, Farrell wrote nearly 600 stories for the magazine market. His earliest Western fiction tended to stress action and gun play, but increasingly his stories began to focus on characters in historical situations and the problems faced by those characters. *Follow the New Grass* (1954) was Farrell's first Western novel, a story concerned with a desperate battle over grazing rights in the Cheyenne Indian reserve. It was followed by *West with the Missouri* (1955), an exciting story of riverboats, gamblers, and gunmen. *Fort Deception* (1960), *Ride the Wild Country* (1963), *The Renegade* (1970), and *The Devil's Playground* (1976) are among the best of Farrell's later Western novels. *Desperate Journey*, a first collection of Cliff Farrell's Western short stories, has also been published.

SANTA FE WAGON BOSS

Cliff Farrell

GUNSMOKE

First published by Doubleday

This hardback edition 2005
by BBC Audiobooks Ltd
by arrangement with
Golden West Literary Agency

ISBN 1 4056 8023 7

British Library Cataloguing in Publication Data available.

Printed and bound in Great Britain by
Antony Rowe Ltd., Chippenham, Wiltshire

1 ★ SANTA FE was more than three hundred miles astern, and Hays City lay two hundred miles ahead, with the waterless Jornada still to be crossed, as Alex Briscoe and his three men camped their two wagons in concealment half a day's journey below that point that freighting men knew as the middle springs of the Cimarron River.

They built a tiny cook fire. The thin dawn of the new day lighted the brush as they cooked their food. They had traveled all night, picking their own trail in the moonlight for the high-wheeled prairie wagons whose canvas hoods loomed above them. They used only dry twigs for the fire, and shielded the small glow with wagon sheets and blankets hung on wheels and stakes.

For this was buffalo country, and the spear hunters of half a dozen tribes made meat in this region.

And it was also scalp country in this year, 1869.

"We'll hit the lower spring come daybreak tomorrow, with luck," Alex estimated. "Fort Dodge in a week, and Hays in two weeks."

He reached to straighten the smoke-blackened coffeepot, which began to tilt as it sat boiling on the embers.

As he did so, rifles and pistols opened up from the brush around them. Something like the slap of a brutal hand struck him in the right side. It was a bullet from a rifle, and it had been aimed at the middle of his back at the moment of his sudden shift of position.

But he did not know that, or what had happened. The impact drove all consciousness out of him with a black rush and he pitched forward alongside the fire, the coffee spilling into the embers.

The guns kept roaring. Around him his three comrades were dying. He lay stretched face down with the first glow of the coming sun lighting the sky.

Presently someone kicked him over on his back and looked down at him and said, "It's Briscoe, all right, and he's cashed in, too."

He aroused later and dully noted that the sun was straight overhead and that he seemed to be in a moving wagon. He drifted off again. Ages afterwards he became aware of events

1

once more. It was sundown. He finally knew he was lying, legs doubled, in a wagon, cramped among other objects.

Next he became aware that these objects around him were the bodies of men. Dead men! His own companions who had been sitting with him at the cook fire. Horror now drove some of the inertia out of him.

It all began to come back. He was Alex Briscoe, wagonmaster and principal owner of the honored Santa Fe freighting firm of Briscoe & Company. He had left Santa Fe with two wagons . . .

The treasure! The bullion and the gold that his wagons had carried!

Now he remembered everything. Outside he heard voices occasionally, speaking in the stilted, terse syllables of men whose nerves are on edge.

The wagons had halted. Darkness had come. Then he became aware of fire! Flames were breaking out beneath the wagon in which he lay. Dry brush had been heaped there and touched off. Thin tongues of flame were flickering through the openings in the wagon bed.

He tried to arise. He fought the stiff, clinging arms of a dead man who seemed to want to hold him down. It was Bill Stoker a man with whom he had traveled down the trail to Santa Fe many times.

He managed to twist free of Bill Stoker's ghostly grasp and rise to his knees. Smoke and heat gagged him. The canvas hood was beginning to burn.

He lifted himself to his feet. He knew they would kill him if they discovered he was still alive. He heard a whip pop and someone barked, "Hike!" The other of his two wagons was creaking into motion.

He realized that all of the bullion had been removed from the wagon in which he stood. He reeled to the rear of the vehicle, pulled himself over the high bow, and dropped to the ground.

None of them were in sight. He landed in a burning tuft of grass, but rolled clear and into the darkness of the thin brush, and that action extinguished his smoldering shirt. He kept rolling farther away from the flaming wagon.

He lay gazing through the brush. The other wagon was lurching away through the sandy dry wash. With it rode four men on saddle horses, driving ahead of them the six loose harness animals that had been attached to the burning vehicle.

The four riders were naked to the waist, and had dabbed

2

their skins with red clay and wore feathers. Alex saw one of them plainly, and saw the brands on the horses that two of them rode. Then they were gone into the darkness.

Blood flowed from his reopened wound. A great apathy crept upon him. It would be so easy to merely lie here.

Then he forced himself to begin crawling.

2 ★ IT WAS more than two weeks later, and early darkness was deepening, when he rode into view of the lights of Hays City on the Kansas border. These lights became a glowing oasis amid the blackness of the prairie as he passed the army post, forded the creek, and came into full view of the settlement.

He had borrowed a horse and also a holstered pistol at Fort Dodge on the Arkansas River. The horse now aroused to the knowledge that surcease from the fast miles was at hand, but his own body did not respond.

He thought of his dead comrades beyond the Jornada, and the lost bullion. Three months previously, prosperous and sure of himself, he had left Hays City for Santa Fe with his freight wagons. He was returning, half starved, ragged and carrying a partly healed bullet wound, and bringing news of impending bankruptcy to his partner.

He brought a hand smashing down on his thigh with gusty impact. He blamed himself for not anticipating what had happened.

The lights came nearer, and he could make out the refrain of a hurdy-gurdy in a dance hall. Somewhere a shrill soprano was singing. A woman screamed laughingly and wantonly amid the tents and sodhouses which fringed the more substantial core of the town.

Sparks and wood smoke plumed from the scuttle stack of a locomotive in the new Kansas Pacific yards. He crossed a spur track which was still unballasted and gazed at a white and black painted sign which jutted above the ridgepole of a sizable warehouse.

SHANNON SOUTHWESTERN
FREIGHTING

Big corrals flanked the structure. In these, horses, mules,

and oxen drowsed. The bare hoops of idle freight wagons showed above the yard fence. Lamplight glowed in the office.

Driven by the rage that had been in him all these days, Alex rode nearer. Only Barney Shannon's night hostler sat in the office, smoking a pipe, feet cocked on a desk.

Pausing his horse out of reach of the beam of light, he shouted, "Where's Len Capehart?"

The hostler's feet came down, and he scanned the shadows, blinking. "At Char Shannon's house, I reckon," he responded.

"So he's back from Santa Fe?" Alex said as though that confirmed something.

"He's back," the hostler snorted. "But he's not to be bothered by the likes o' you, whoever you are. He's goin' to a champagne supper. Real sporty."

Satisfied with what he had learned, Alex rode onward. He passed cattle pens and loading chutes and army warehouses that were being built in preparation for the coming campaign against the Indians.

From the depths of the town someone fired a pistol twice in the air. Afterwards, riders, whooping good-naturedly, rode out of Hays. These were Texas trail men, heading back to their wagons after a round of the saloons. The wind brought the pungent, wild animal tang peculiar to longhorns. Trail herds, and their accompanying chuck wagons, were bedded around the town.

He passed a varnished private parlor car on a side track near the depot. Velvet draperies, held by gold cords, framed the windows. White-coated waiters were preparing a table agleam with fine linen and silver. Champagne buckets stood ready.

All this luxury, Alex reflected, and a man's scalp was still not safe a mile beyond town.

The arrival of rails at Hays had brought other items of civilization, along with parlor cars. The settlement swarmed with bullwhackers and mule skinners from the Santa Fe Trail, with buckskin-clad buffalo hunters, and with Mexican cargadores from as far as Chihuahua, with Texas drovers from beyond the Brazos, with gamblers, and fandango women from the brothels of eastern cities.

And Wild Bill Hickok was town marshal, with orders to maintain law and peace.

All of the big Santa Fe freighting companies had shifted their headquarters to the new railhead from Abilene and

Independence. Alex rode past his own yards and saw Dan Foss, his night man, sitting in his usual place in a barrel chair at the entrance of the barn tunnel. Dan was puffing a pipe. Alex's office was dark and locked. Hoxie Carver, his yard boss, had gone home for the night.

Alex smiled tautly at the thought of Dan Foss sitting there so peacefully each night while he, Alex Briscoe, wounded and wild with thirst, had fought his way through those burning miles on foot across the Jornada, with the dust of Kiowan and Arapahoe hunters lifting on the prairie, and with the knowledge of disaster so monstrous in his mind and with the need for vengeance burning in him even greater than his thirst.

This was the first time he had smiled in weeks, and that was a blessing, for it brought rationality back to him. He realized then how close to the edge of physical limitation he had been. Twenty-eight years of age, he stood within a fraction of six feet and normally weighed one hundred and eighty pounds of sinew and brawn, though he had lost more than ten of those pounds since that morning on the Cimarron. He was days overdue on a shave, and his hair, very dark and very thick, curled over the collar of his flannel shirt.

His eyes were dark and set beneath square brows. He had rough-hewn chin and mouth and nose, and the carriage of a self-sufficient man. He had never before felt the need of asking help of anyone. But he needed help now. His wound had bled many times, and his blood-stiffened shirt was a torture to him.

He passed the barns and yards of Morgan Webb's Overland Transport. He saw Webb sitting at his desk in the office, working on ledgers. Webb, a handsome, deep-chested man with pale, prematurely graying hair, wore formal evening dress. Pearl studs gleamed in his pleated linen shirt. A fine surrey, with a matched team of pacers, stood in harness at the door.

Alex thought of going to Morg Webb for help, but he now saw another man in the office. This one was a stranger who wore a brace of pistols. That decided him, and he rode on into the darkness.

He presently slid woodenly from the saddle in the shadows near a two-story, gray-painted residence which his partner, Ellis Thayer, had built as a home for himself and his wife.

He tied up the horse in darkness. The hour was still so early the curtains had not been drawn in the kitchen. Amelia

Thayer, Ellis's wife was alone there, finishing the supper dishes. Alex watched her empty the dishpan into the drain trough, then dry it and hang it out of sight. She removed the crisp gingham apron she was wearing and glanced into a small mirror as she touched her rich brown hair.

The kitchen was pin-neat, with every utensil polished and hanging on its peg. The maple floor gleamed with wax. He could see into the parlor through the small intervening hall. A lamp with a pink china shade burned there on a marble stand alongside a brass-bound Bible. Its light rested comfortably on a brocaded sofa and on stiff-backed, stuffed chairs with needlepoint covers and antimacassars as white as snow. There were hooked rugs on the floor and water colors on the wall and painted cups in the racks. All these were Amelia's handiwork.

She was perhaps thirty-five, a shapely, firm-bosomed, comely-featured woman, with good hips and slender waist and throat. She had calm brown eyes, and wore a dress that was modest and precisely fitted. She had made the dress herself.

It seemed to Alex that Amelia Thayer was as changeless and even-rhythmed as the contents of the hymn books he had often seen her carrying to choir practice. She was twenty years younger than Ellis, whom she had married a few years in the past.

He moved to the door, tapped softly, and said, with his lips close to the panel, "It's Alex Briscoe, Amelia."

She came swiftly and the door opened. She uttered a small sound as she took in his gaunt face and alkali-streaked garb and the dark stain on the skirt of his saddle jacket. He stepped in, closed the door, then moved to the window and drew the gingham curtains tight. He stood listening. The house was very silent.

"Where's Ellis?" he asked.

"He's—he's out somewhere in town," Amelia said. "He often goes for a walk. Alex! Merciful heaven! You look terrible! Starved! And you're hurt! There's blood on——"

"Bullet wound, but it happened many days ago. Would you mind helping me off with this coat, Amelia?"

He remembered that she could not bear the sight of blood. Now she forced herself to do this thing. With her aid he escaped from the duck saddle jacket. He saw the wan hue of her face as she gazed at his shirt, which only partly covered the stained bandage that he had contrived.

6

"I'll need water to soak off the shirt and bandage," he said. "I can manage it!"

"You need a doctor," she said shakily. "I'll go and——"

"No," he said. "This isn't as bad as it looks. I've lived with it for a long time. It won't kill me now."

"But——!" she murmured. Then she was silent, her color coming and going as she fought this out with her concepts of modesty.

She left the kitchen and returned bearing bandage material, a medicine chest, and scissors and thread.

"Stand by the table," she said, and avoided his eyes.

He unbuckled his gun belt and laid it on the table. Once again he listened to the silence of the house. The only sound was the snip of the scissors as Amelia cut away his shirt.

He felt her fingers recoil a little at each contact with him. She was fighting a hard battle with her timidity, and she was shaking visibly as she bared him to the waist. As with all physically active men, he looked much larger thus. His shoulders were wide and smoothly muscled. His skin was lightly tanned by a plains sun that burned even through a shirt. The curving scar of an old knife wound ran across his right upper chest. There was a pucker of a bullet injury on his left shoulder. A Confederate rifle ball had given him that souvenir at Antietam. Just below it was the ragged mark where a Kiowan war lance had glanced.

Amelia's fingers tested the blood-stiffened resistance of the bandage which clung to his flesh. He winced.

"I could use a drink, Amelia," he said.

"You know I'm opposed to the use of spirits, Alex," she said, and there was no compromise with her principles in her voice even in this emergency. "I've set coffee on the stove to warm, and also what is left of a meat stew, and that will be better for you."

She worked for a moment. "What happened?" she asked. "Ellis received a letter from you by the only mail that has come through from Santa Fe since the Indian outbreak. You said you had something big in mind."

He lost his breath as she worked the bandage free, exposing the bullet injury along his side. "We were ambushed on the Cimarron," he finally was able to say. "I'm all that's left."

"All that's left?" she breathed. "Who were with you?"

"Bill Stoker, Hugh Appleton, Tim Ryon. They've worked for Briscoe & Company for years. They're gone. Dead, and burned. And two wagons and two teams lost!"

She was ashen. She stood staring at him as though her thoughts were racing to something else. "Indians?" she asked hollowly.

"They were dressed like Indians."

Her gaze searched his face. "They were white men," he said, and nodded. "Disguised. They thought I was dead, along with the others. They piled all four of our bodies in one wagon. Then they drove miles off the trail to a place where no one would ever likely stumble on the ashes. They set fire to the wagon. But I came out of it in time to get away unseen."

"Why—why would men do such a thing?" she choked. "What—what became of the other wagon?"

"They had loaded all the bullion and money into it and drove it away," Alex said.

"Bullion? Money?"

"I told Ellis in my letter that I was negotiating for a shipment at Santa Fe that would bring a big profit," he said. "I told him not to mention the details. I got the contract. I signed to deliver one hundred and fifty thousand dollars' worth of coin and bullion to the express company and banks here in Hays. It had been accumulating for weeks in the safes of the banks and trading outfits at Santa Fe. They were anxious to transfer it to the States. There was some gold, but the bulk was in Mexican bullion. It was stored in heavy iron boxes with three or four big Mexican padlocks on each box. All in all, it weighed around two tons. The stage company refused to guarantee delivery because of the Indian situation. So I took the gamble."

"Gamble?"

"I was sure I could get through by dividing the load between two wagons so that we could make fast tracks," he said. "We traveled at night and avoided the stretch of trail where the Indians watch for caravans. I agreed to deliver the shipment in sixty days. We were to receive a seven per cent premium above the usual rates for insuring it."

"Insuring?" Amelia exclaimed, "Oh, Alex!"

"All freighting is a gamble, Amelia," he said. "We stood to earn about twelve thousand dollars on that one haul. We're cleaned out instead."

"Cleaned out?"

"I pledged title to Briscoe & Company as security for the treasure. I posted a bond. Our assets, at best, were only worth about two thirds the value of the bullion, but the shippers assumed that much of the risk. However, they won't realize half of the company's real value at forced sale. Maybe fifty thousand dollars. Ellis and I will still owe around a hundred thousand dollars."

"A hundred thousand . . . ? That's impossible!"

"Unless we get the bullion back in a hurry."

"Back!" she exclaimed. "You think you have a chance to . . . ?"

"Two chances. I recognized one of the bunch that bushwhacked us. The next day I found some food that was still eatable in the ashes of the wagon. That saved me. I made it on foot across the Jornada to the Arkansas. I got a horse and a gun at Fort Dodge."

Amelia finished treating his injury and applied a bandage. Then she placed food on the table.

"Do you want to tell me the name of the man you recognized?" she asked hesitantly.

"Grassman," Alex said. "Bart Grassman. He's a tough teamster who has worked for one outfit or another for years."

"You mentioned you had two chances. . . ."

"The other is Len Capehart," he said.

"Capehart? That gun fighter? Char Shannon's wagon boss!"

"I understand he's here in Hays City tonight," Alex said. "He was in Santa Fe when I headed up the trail with the bullion. Any idea when he pulled into town?"

"Why—why, several days ago, I believe. He took a chance and rushed a few Shannon wagons and stock through from Santa Fe. Ellis talked to him. He said you had pulled out of Santa Fe just ahead of him, but he saw no sign of you on the trail. He didn't mention the treasure."

"My trip with the bullion was supposed to be a secret, but every freighting boss in Santa Fe knew about it," Alex said. "Capehart among them. In fact, he tried to bid in the job for Shannon Southwestern, but I had already closed the deal."

He looked at Amelia. "There are a couple of other items. Grassman was working as a hostler for Shannon Southwestern at Santa Fe. More than that, he and his pals were riding horses that bore the Diamond S brand. I saw the brand plainly on at least two horses."

"Diamond S?"

"That's the company brand Barney Shannon uses on all the livestock he owns," Alex said. "I want to ask Capehart a few questions. And Barney Shannon, also."

"Alex!" Amelia exclaimed. "Surely you must know that Barney Shannon is dead."

Alex whirled on her. "Dead? I didn't know."

"He died one night last spring. He dropped dead right in his wagon yard, in fact. There had been a fire at his barns. It started in three places at once. But they put it out before it really got going. Two wagons were destroyed and some damage done to a freight shed. But the excitement was too much for Barney Shannon. That and the overexertion. It was his heart. He just keeled over."

Alex realized she was no longer meeting his gaze frankly. "You say three fires broke out? Are you trying to say they were set—that someone tried to burn down . . . ?"

He was watching the changing expression in Amelia. "When did this take place?" he asked.

"The—the next night after you—you had left for Santa Fe with the spring caravan. They never found out who started the fire."

"I see," Alex said slowly. "They think I might have backtracked long enough to put a torch to Shannon Southwestern. They're holding me responsible for Barney Shannon's death."

"Some people will think anything," she said.

"You're not so sure about me yourself, are you, Amelia?" His voice was harsh.

"Don't pick a quarrel with me, Alex," she said without anger. "I'm your friend. But I can't control the thinking of others. Everyone knows that your father and Barney Shannon were bitter enemies."

Her voice softened. "You must realize that you are a violent man also, Alex," she said gently. "Like Len Capehart, you have a reputation for being fast with your pistol and your fists. I never fullly realized how rough your life had been until I saw your body just now." Her color deepened. "Those scars! This gunshot you received beyond the Jornada was not your first experience with such things."

Alex said, "No, it was not, Amelia." He donned one of Ellis's shirts which she had provided, slid stiffly into his stained saddle jacket, and reached for his gun belt.

"Don't misunderstand me, Alex," she said. "I abhor fighting and the hardness of some of your ways, but I know that it probably is unavoidable in your profession. I don't believe you had anything to do with what happened that night. But what I believe and what Charlotte Shannon believes are different matters. Char is Barney Shannon's only child. She thinks like him. It is a strange situation that you and she should find yourselves partners at a time like this."

Alex swung around, staring at her. "Partners? What are you saying, Amelia?"

She made a helpless gesture. "How can I tell you? You'll take it wrong. But the truth is that my husband sold his interest in your freighting company to Charlotte Shannon more than a week ago. She's a full partner in Briscoe & Company."

"Sold? Sold to Char Shannon?" The shock of that moved numbly through him.

"Char offered Ellis twenty thousand dollars," Amelia said apologetically. "With the railroad building toward Colorado, Ellis fears for the future of wagon freighting. He couldn't turn down the opportunity."

"But Ellis couldn't—wouldn't sell without talking it over with me," Alex said disbelievingly. "Not—not to a Shannon, of all people!"

"He was afraid if he waited until you got back from Santa Fe that she would withdraw the offer," Amelia said.

"But—but—it isn't possible! I can't believe it! And only twenty thousand dollars. Why a one-third partnership in Briscoe & Company was worth a lot more than that."

"In theory, perhaps. But this was cash. It assures us of a comfortable living, Alex. You can see that."

Alex suddenly laughed, and this time there was high irony in him. "Char Shannon bought bankruptcy when she bought into Briscoe & Company," he said.

"Bankruptcy?"

"As partner she's liable for that lost bullion also. Under the law a partner, no matter what proportion he owns in the firm, is equally liable for debts. Even Shannon Southwestern can't stand a jolt of that size. It'll go under, along with Briscoe."

Then a new thought sobered him. "But Len Capehart wouldn't have put Grassman up to robbing wagons in which Char had a partnership," he said slowly.

"It could have been a case of the left hand not knowing what the right hand was doing," Amelia pointed out. "You two have been out of communication with Hays for months. You didn't even know Barney Shannon was dead. I doubt if Capehart did either, for both of you went down the trail with the spring caravan. And he probably didn't know Char had bought out my husband's share of your company. Then again . . ."

She hesitated. "Perhaps Capehart saw a chance to feather his own nest," she went on with a shrug. "Perhaps he feels that he should look out for his own interests."

"He's been with Shannon Southwestern a long time," he said dubiously. "He was with Barney Shannon even before the war. Barney Shannon trusted him."

"Even loyalty may have its price," Amelia said. "One hundred and fifty thousand dollars is quite a temptation."

He turned to the door. She barred his path. "You still intend to confront him?" she asked protestingly.

"And Char Shannon," he said. "I want to see the expression on her face when she learns she bought a pig in a poke."

She caught his arm. "Don't be foolish, Alex! Capehart will laugh at you and deny everything. What else can he do? It—it might end up in a shooting."

"So it might."

"But he's a gun fighter!" she exclaimed. "Don't be rash, Alex!"

"Three men were murdered out there," he said. "They were friends of mine. You don't ask me to forget that, do you?"

She saw there was no deterring him. Her hand dropped away.

She stood motionless as he went out and closed the door. She remained in that position with an absorption that was almost feline in its intensity. She strained her ears to identify each small sound which came back.

She knew when Alex reached his horse and she marked the faint creak of leather as he mounted. Then he was riding away. She continued to wait until she was certain he would not return.

Then she walked into the small hall and mounted the carpeted stairs to a bedroom above. The oil lamp had been dimmed to a faint glow which did not penetrate the drawn window curtains. She turned up the wick a trifle and the light strengthened. On the stand beside the lamp stood an empty whiskey bottle.

Her husband lay stretched on the bed. He was fully dressed, and he aroused now, blinking. He sat up and said thickly, "Oh, it's you, dear?"

Amelia gazed at him for a long time without speaking. There was no tangible expression in her small, handsome face. Her eyes, a dark amber hue in this light, were equally unreadable.

Ellis had struck a windfall when he had bought an interest

in Briscoe & Company a few years in the past. Tom Briscoe's fortunes had fallen to low ebb at that time, due to the breaking out of the Civil War and the ensuing guerrilla raids along the Santa Fe trail. Alex was gone, fighting on the Union side. His father had reluctantly been forced to sell a one-third partnership in the company to Ellis Thayer for a paltry five thousand dollars.

But before the war ended, the Santa Fe trade had bounded back, and Briscoe & Company had bounded with it. Ellis soon had his investment paid and doubled. It was during this upswing that Amelia married him. She was the widow of a storekeeper, whom she had married at eighteen, and whose death had left her penniless at twenty-five. She had been supporting herself by tutoring backward school pupils and giving singing lessons.

Not many days in the past Ellis had been his usual affable, rather pompous, self-important, russet-cheeked self. He was not a freighting man, and had let Alex carry the responsibility of the company since Tom Briscoe's death, while he lived the life of a gentleman of means.

Now he was a man suddenly tumbling to ruin. His eyes were bloodshot and pouched. His mouth had loosened into moist weakness. His features were blurred—as though he were uncertain of his own beliefs. There was latent fear in him.

"I—I must have fallen asleep, dear," he said. "I thought I heard voices in the kitchen a while ago."

"Alex Briscoe was here," she said. And added, "As you well know!"

"Alex? Why, I——!"

"That's why you stayed so quiet," Amelia went on, and there was a cold, scornful bite in her voice. "You weren't asleep. You were never wider awake in your life."

She kept looking at him in that icy way. "So that's why you sold in such a hurry to Char Shannon," she said, and it was as though he weren't even present. "So that's why you and —and——"

She decided against saying any more. They kept looking at each other. Ellis Thayer's clouded eyes became frightened and turned away.

3 ★ ALEX DISMOUNTED and tethered his horse to an ornamental hitching post in front of the Shannon home, which stood a block or more west of the Hartley residence. Barney Shannon had built a sizable, comfortable home for himself and his daughter. A deep veranda faced the street, with vines climbing the posts. Flowers and sapling trees stood inside the wrought-iron fence. It was the most pretentious house in the town. Barney Shannon had always tried to make a better appearance than his neighbors—or his competitors.

Lights gleamed in all the windows. These windows were open to admit the cooling night breeze after the heat of the day, and he heard a girl humming the refrain of a rather bold song that had been popular among the troops of both sides during the war. That was Charlotte Shannon's voice. She had the reputation of kicking up her heels at the rigid demands of convention.

He entered the gate, walked through the warm darkness up the brick path onto the porch, and twisted the brass key on the doorbell. Heavy padding footsteps sounded, and the door was opened by a short and very rotund Osage Indian woman. Her name was Anna Whitehorse, and she had been Charlotte Shannon's nurse and attendant since childhood.

Startled, the Indian woman hastily tried to slam the door, but he placed a palm against the portal, holding it open. "I want to talk to Miss Charlotte, Anna," he said. "Go tell her I'm here before I take a lodgepole to you."

The Indian woman's broad brown face was hostile. She glared disparagingly at his trail-worn garb and unshaven jaws. "Missy Char busy. She no got time talk you tonight."

"She'll have to take the time," he said. "Now go find her, or do you want me to do it for you?"

A step sounded in the background and a man came into the reception hall from the parlor. "Well, well!" he exclaimed.

"Hello, Capehart," Alex said.

"It really is you, Briscoe," Len Capehart said. "I recognized your voice."

"I came to see Char Shannon," Alex said. "But our bar-

14

rel-shaped friend here seems to think that my appearance leaves something to be desired."

Capehart laughed. "She may have a point there. But it's all right, Anna. We'll dust out the place after he leaves."

The Osage woman grunted in disgust, gave Alex a glare, and moved unwillingly away.

Capehart ushered him into the parlor. This room was comfortably furnished with easy chairs and sofas done in grain leather. The waxed cedar floor was strewn with Indian and Mexican rugs and a magnificent cougar pelt. The usual clutter of bric-a-brac, in the fashion of the time, was missing—further evidence that Char Shannon carried an independent viewpoint.

"We've been doing some worrying about you, Briscoe," Capehart said.

"Worrying?"

"You're long overdue from Santa Fe. We've been fearin' that you had maybe hit bad trouble."

Len Capehart was a lithely-framed man with flat, strong shoulders. He was lean, and was as brown and pliable as well-tanned rawhide. He had been born in Tennessee, and the softness of the South ran in his voice. He had never mentioned it, but Alex happened to know that he had fought through the war wearing a gray uniform with Jeb Stuart's cavalry.

Capehart had the coolest eyes Alex had ever seen. Stone gray. His forehead was intelligently high, his features sensitively cut. He was clean-shaven, with light brown hair, and had the poise of a man who carved his own thoughts and formed his own dreams—a man who would stay with a cause once he had dedicated himself to it.

He was dressed with unusual formality in a dark store suit, with a white shirt and a low starched collar with a carefully knotted dark string tie. The bulge of his holster was only slightly perceptible beneath the skirt of the coat. He was never without his pistol, to Alex's knowledge. As wagonmaster of Barney Shannon's freighting company he had been a stern disciplinarian, forcing his will on the wild teamsters and bullwhackers, who respected only a man tougher than themselves. He had acquired far more than his share of enemies.

"Mosey upstairs, Anna," Capehart said, "an' tell Miss Char that Alex Briscoe has showed up at last. She'll be right interested, I'm sure."

Capehart's searching gaze returned. "What happened,

Briscoe? You left Santa Fe ahead o' me, but I been home nigh onto a week. You had a rough trip, by the looks."

"Yes," Alex said. "But you seem to have had it a lot smoother."

Capehart frowned a little and weighed the meaning of that remark. "We had four wagons an' considerable livestock hung up at Santa Fe which I knew was needed back at our yards here in Hays," he said. "So I decided to follow your example an' try to luck it through by makin' fast tracks an' travelin' off the trail. Fact is, we walked right in your prints for a while. We was travelin' empty an' faster. Figured you didn't want company, so we swung north of the slant you was takin' toward the Cimarron. We should have reached the river about the same time as you, but we was quite a ways upstream. It was on the Cimarron that we had our only real trouble. Horse-stealin' Indians stampeded our remuda at night. I got most o' the stuff back, but that country is alive with huntin' parties this year. A man who goes out there is takin' a real chance of losin' part of his hair."

"Yes," Alex said. "I took a chance. I still have my scalp, but I came out loser, nevertheless. Can you prove you were with your wagons all the time, Capehart?"

Capehart's gaze thinned and he moved back a pace. That would give him more room to draw his pistol if the need came. "Now why would I have to prove it?" he asked.

A young woman came rushing into the room and placed herself between them. "I'll take care of this, Len," she said. "I heard what he said. The Briscoes always were trouble-makers, but there never was a day when the Shannons couldn't handle them."

Alex found himself facing dark eyes that were very large and very clear, and also exceedingly scornful. He had crossed trails with Charlotte Shannon many times, but had never been at such close quarters with her before. Because of the bitterness between their fathers he had, from childhood, pointedly gone out of his way to avoid her. And she had ignored him with a swish of the hem of her skirt.

However, she had never been a person who could be easily overlooked. As a youngster she had been a button-eyed bundle of freckled activity, leading her playmates in mischief in the streets and wagon yards at St. Joe and Independence.

After her mother's death she had been permitted by her father to travel each summer down the trail to far and exotic New Mexico. Alex had vivid memories of her, a willowy girl of fourteen, at that crossroads between slender childhood

16

and ripening, curving beauty, standing in the shade of her father's huge, canvas-hooded wagons in the ancient plaza at Santa Fe, her calico skirt pinned tight around her booted legs while she swung a bullwhip in competition with whiskered veterans of the trail, snapping deerflies off the rumps of oxen without disturbing the animals. The glances she had cast in his direction in those days had been as withering as the look with which she was now trying to crush him.

When she was sixteen, her father had bundled her away into the care of relatives in the East for refining and gentling. She was twenty-four now and had not married, although Alex knew it was not because of lack of suitors.

He found himself at a distinct disadvantage. For one thing, she was a vitally attractive, raven-haired young woman who was endowed with a full complement of physical charms. In the second place, she wore an evening gown which seemed to be calculated, in his opinion, to call attention to these attractions. The dress, white and filmy, was revealing of shoulder and bosom.

Her skin was tanned a healthy golden hue. She had arranged her hair high, making her seem taller. She was tilting her small nose a trifle in a gesture that he remembered. Her lips, moist and full, were pursed scornfully. Her hands were small and capable and bore a deeper tan—the mark of a horsewoman. Evidently she still preferred spirited mounts which required precise handling.

"I can still swing a bullwhip too," she sniffed, as though defining his thoughts.

It was the dress that offended Alex! He had been brought up to be strait-laced in matters of feminine attire. He let his glance travel critically up and down her a second time.

She endured this smolderingly. "Well!" she challenged. "I paid a pretty price for this dress, and now you don't seem to like it."

"Every cent of it shows." He nodded.

"Ha! You think it's too skimpy, don't you? I'm branded as a wicked woman."

"I came here to——" Alex began.

"Just a moment. It's only fair I get a chance to take a second look at you my friend. After all, you're no prize beauty either. That shirt looks like you stole it off a clothesline. It's sizes too small. And, at least, I've had a bath lately. How about you? How long has it been since you've been inside a barbershop?"

"I had to pass up every one between the Cimarron and

Hays," Alex said. "The trouble is they're run by men who cut a little close. They use scalping knives."

They stood eye to eye, neither giving an inch. Just what had started the feud between their fathers was a mystery to Alex. It dated back, he knew, to before his and Char Shannon's births—to the early days of the Santa Fe trade.

Toughest competitor to Tom Briscoe and his freighting company had always been Barney Shannon and his Shannon Southwestern outfit. Barney Shannon sought to monopolize the trading and wagon-freighting business between the border and the New Mexican frontier. Redheaded, bearded, rock-fisted, he had been a man whose ambition was to dominate.

But he had never been able to dominate Tom Briscoe. Nor had he succeeded in driving Briscoe & Company out of business. The Briscoes, first the father, and then the son, had fought him toe to toe, on equal terms.

But there had been more than a clash of personalities between the two older men. Some deeper issue, something that had colored their lives, had been involved.

Alex's father had never mentioned the real reason why he and Barney Shannon had opposed each other so unyielding-ly. Tom Briscoe had been in his grave more than three years. He had been killed by an Apache arrow in a fight near Wagon Mound and had taken the secret with him. And now Barney Shannon was also dead and Alex was at swordspoint with his daughter.

"At least Briscoe an' me see eye to eye in one matter." Capehart spoke. "You're only about a whoop an' a holler from bein' half naked, Char."

"You ought to see what they're wearing back East, where this dress came from," she said. "I'm practically muffled in a horse blanket by comparison. But we're drifting far off the subject. I still want Mr. Briscoe to explain what he meant by that question he asked you, Len."

"I understand you and I are partners, Miss Shannon," Alex said.

She nodded warily. "Yes. Any objections?"

"I take it for granted that you're planning on offering to buy out my share of Briscoe & Company also," Alex said.

She shook her head. "No."

"Why not? I imagine you'd jump at the chance to get the name of Briscoe out of the freighting business forever."

"A partnership was all that was necessary." Char Shannon

shrugged. "Conditions are changing in wagon freighting, as you know. We must change with it. Right at the moment, the railroad is asking for bids on grading two hundred miles of line west into Colorado. The work won't start until spring, but it will be profitable to anyone who gets the job at the right figure. Shannon Southwestern is bidding. In addition, the Army is finding out that it underestimated the strength of the Indians, and that the campaign will extend into next year at least, and perhaps longer, and that it will need help from civilian freighters and packers. We intend to go after that business also."

"And so . . . ?" Alex questioned.

"To handle contracts of that size will require more stock and equipment than Shannon has available," she said. "Both the railroad and the Army will be more inclined to award the work to a company it knows is able to fulfill its agreement on time. By combining Briscoe & Company with mine we will be in a position to take care of everything. Therefore I grabbed at the chance when Ellis Thayer came to me and offered to sell his share of your company."

Alex started to interrupt her, but decided against it. He took it for granted she was not telling the truth about Ellis's having initiated the deal, but thought it better to give her more rope.

He was avoiding coming to the real purpose of his visit, which was to reveal that she was facing ruin. He wanted to keep her talking so that he could watch Capehart for signs of knowledge of what he was going to say.

"So you needed more livestock and equipment to carry out your plans?" he said. "What about me? Am I included with the livestock?"

"We'll merge your company with Shannon Southwestern, if that is satisfactory to you," Char Shannon said calmly. "You will have charge of the freighting end of the business for the combined firms. Len will look after the grading job if it is awarded to us."

"Just what do you mean by 'we'?"

"It is a collective term meaning Shannon Southwestern," she explained. "Dad left the company to me in its entirety."

"I just learned about your father's death," Alex said. "I was told it was from exertion after someone set fire to his barns."

Char Shannon's face lost color. She said, "Yes," but the word was low and without expression.

19

"I also understand that certain persons are convinced I am the man responsible. Are you one of those, Miss Shannon?"

Her lips were gray and quivering a trifle. "Would I have bought a partnership with a man I believed guilty of a thing like that?" she asked.

Alex drew a long breath. "I wondered myself," he admitted. "I must say that your answer surprises me."

"I was never taught to hate the Briscoes as you evidently were brought up to hate the Shannons," she said.

"On the contrary, I was never taught anything about the Shannons," he snapped. "In fact, the name was never mentioned to me. But I was told that your father dropped dead only a day or two after I had pulled out for Santa Fe with the big string last spring. Seems as though some folks figure I backtracked long enough to fire the wagon yard."

"It would have been possible." Char nodded, her voice level. "You were absent from the wagon train on a buffalo hunt for a day and a night and part of another day at that time. That would have been long enough to have made it to Hays and back."

"You seem to have taken steps to check up on me," Alex said grimly.

"I was with the big string, remember." Len Capehart spoke. "I gave her that information."

Alex kept gazing at Char. "But you don't think I did it?"

"No," she said, adding nothing to that terse word.

Alex looked at Capehart. "How about you? Do you think I sneaked back to Hays that night?"

"I haven't decided one way or another." Capehart shrugged. "When I do I'll let you know—also one way or another." He paused. There was a run of steel beneath the softness in his voice when he spoke again. "Yes, sir, I'll certainly let you know, Briscoe."

Alex's glance returned to Char Shannon. "You were talking of merging my company with Shannon Southwestern," he said. "What are your terms?"

"You will be a partner in the merged company, in proportion to the value of your holdings," she said. "If we win this grading contract, I propose that we take payment in stock in the railroad. We hope to take on other grading contracts under the same arrangement in the future, not only with the Kansas Pacific but other railroads. A line that calls itself the Atchison, Topeka & Santa Fe is organizing to build westward up the Arkansas River and onward into Colorado and perhaps to California. We hope to get a share of that business also when it really starts work."

She added, "In that way Shannon Southwestern will gradually shift to railroading as the need for wagon freighting lessens. It is the plan my father had laid out, and I am following it. And you will profit with us, of course."

"Provided I'm not hung for causing Barney Shannon's death in the meantime," Alex said. "By having me close at hand your friend here perhaps hopes I'll furnish the excuse he needs to put a rope around my neck."

Len Capehart took a step forward, but Char Shannon pushed him back. "See to it then that you don't give him that excuse," she said.

"The name of the merged firm will be Briscoe & Shannon," Alex said. "Not Shannon Southwestern, as you mentioned."

"Shannon & Briscoe," she said. "After all——"

Alex produced a coin. "Call it," he said, and spun it.

"Heads," Char Shannon called. The coin came down tails. Alex had won.

"The name," he said, "is Briscoe & Shannon. And that is as it should be."

He expected Char Shannon to complain. But, though annoyed and disappointed, she shrugged and said nothing. He found himself nettled. He had not expected her to stand by a gambling agreement.

4 ★ ALEX WAS at a loss. He was certain Char Shannon had no inkling of the disastrous news he had been withholding. He believed she was too volatile, and spoke too frankly, to be able to hide such knowledge.

Capehart was a different proposition. There was no telling what lay behind that tanned, unreadable face. Amelia Thayer probably had hit on the explanation when she had said that Capehart had seized on the chance to enrich himself, and now that he had learned he had perhaps ruined Char he would take every precaution against incriminating himself. Perhaps he had not been remembered in Barney Shannon's will. He had been a powerful factor in the prosperity of Shannon Southwestern, and might feel that he owed no such loyalty to the daughter as he had rendered to the father.

It was easy to attribute many such motives to the taciturn

Tennessean. It was not as easy to make such assumptions stand up. It was plain that Char Shannon not only had implicit confidence in Capehart, but that there was a very firm bond of understanding between them.

It was likely that they were in love. Alex remembered the way she had rushed into the room and angrily defended Capehart against his own implied accusation. That might mean that something deeper than friendship existed between them.

In any event, he realized he had encountered a blank wall at this house as far as uncovering guilty evidence against Capehart was concerned.

Then there was the matter of the whereabouts of Bart Grassman and the others who had participated in the massacre on the Cimarron. Alex realized that he had made a mistake in confronting Capehart and revealing his suspicions of the man's guilt. It was Grassman he must find, above all. Grassman was the real key to the mystery.

Grassman and his followers had been equipped to travel fast when they had pulled away from that desolate spot where they had left Alex supposedly dead with the three bodies in the burning wagon. Each man had his own mount, and they had the teams from both wagons to handle the treasure wagon.

Unless they had met trouble they should have reached Hays days ahead of Alex. If so, the treasure had been divided by this time, no doubt. But Grassman could still be found and made to talk, and the silver and gold might be rounded up.

It was possible Grassman might have decided to double-cross Capehart, and had headed for Texas or the Southwest with the money. In that event Alex realized he might never catch up with them.

But it was more likely they would have headed for the nearest settlements, and that meant the Kansas border. The Cimarron and Arkansas River country was no place in which to linger, with the tribes riding.

No doubt they were all wagon men and therefore well known in Hays, where their presence would not arouse curiosity. But they would need powerful help in disposing of that amount of loot without drawing suspicion. That again brought the finger of circumstantial evidence pointing to Len Capehart.

It occurred to Alex wryly that he had been a trifle vain in
22

quibbling over precedence in the name of a company that was already as good as bankrupt.

He decided to let drop the bombshell. "I am sorry that I am going to be such a great disappointment to you as a partner, Miss Shannon," he said. "But the truth is that the partnership you bought in Briscoe & Company was like buying a dead horse. In fact, it is likely to ruin you."

She stiffened, staring. "What do you mean?"

"You bought into a company that owes one hundred and fifty thousand dollars to clients in Santa Fe," he said. "I lost two wagons carrying bullion and gold, which I had insured under bond, along with the lives of three men. That's why I was overdue. And that is the liability you assumed when you took over Ellis Thayer's share in Briscoe & Company."

He watched her expression shift from disbelief to alarm, and then to consternation. Her emotions were entirely genuine.

Capehart pushed past her, his eyes narrow. "Go on, Briscoe," he said. "Tell it all."

Alex again moved so that the blood-stiffened flap of his saddle jacket swung clear of his holster. He was ready for any action Capehart might make.

Tersely he told of the treasure shipment and the ambush. All color drained from Char Shannon's face.

He told how he had revived to find himself lying among the bullet-torn bodies of his slain crewmen, listening to the crackle of flames as the dry brush that had been piled beneath the wagon was set afire. And of watching the assassins ride away after he had escaped from the wagon.

He withheld some details. He did not mention that he had identified the big, greasy-haired, swarthy Bart Grassman as the leader of the killers. Nor did he reveal that Grassman had been riding a horse wearing the Shannon company's brand.

With a little sighing sound Char abruptly sank down into a chair. Anna Whitehorse, who had been hovering in the background, came hurrying, placed a hand on her wan forehead, then went padding off into the kitchen. She returned with a glass of water. Char pushed this away. "I need something stronger than that, I'm afraid," she said, trying to smile. "If you're telling the truth, Alex Briscoe, this means that—that I stand to lose everything."

"We stand to lose everything," Alex corrected her. "We're partners, remember? I'm in the same boat."

"I scraped bottom to raise the cash to buy out Ellis Thayer," Char said dismally. "I mortgaged this house. I even put up a few pieces of jewelry. The most of it was heirlooms my mother had left to me."

Alex couldn't think of a thing to say. The disaster was more complete than he had anticipated.

Char spoke again, tiredly. "I see now what you were driving at when you started questioning Len about his whereabouts during the trip home from Santa Fe. You think he might have had a hand in what happened to you."

She stared at him with widening eyes. "And I do believe you suspected I may have known about it also."

"I've eliminated you, at least," Alex said. "I admit that I first figured you might have been in on the scheme in order to put Briscoe & Company out of business. I was wrong."

"I'm flattered that you've cleared me as a murder suspect," she said caustically. "Should I thank you?"

"That leaves only me," Capehart said in his velvet drawl.

"Yes," Alex said, his tone equally soft.

There came a flat moment of silence. Char sprang to her feet, frightened, and once more stood between them. "But —but that's utterly ridiculous!" she exclaimed shakily. "What are you up to, Alex Briscoe? It's just as reasonable to say that you did it yourself. Perhaps you killed those men, burned the wagons, and hid the bullion somewhere, then came here with this wild story about being ambushed by men disguised as Indians."

"Why would I do that?" Alex demanded.

"For one hundred and fifty thousand dollars!" she snapped. "And to ruin Shannon Southwestern. You would have money enough to set up another freighting company, and without as much competition."

Capehart placed his hands under her elbows and lifted her bodily aside with ease. "Don't ever stand in front of me again, Char," he said mildly. He looked at Alex. "So that was why you asked if I could prove I was with my wagons all the time?"

"Well?" Alex said unyieldingly.

Capehart shrugged. "I can—with the exception of about twenty-four hours when I was roundin' up the horses the Indians stampeded on the upper Cimarron, as I mentioned."

"Exactly when did this happen?" Alex asked.

Capehart counted on his fingers while he estimated the days. "Almost three weeks ago. Maybe a day or two less. It's right hard to recollect exactly."

24

He studied Alex closely for a moment, then shrugged again, a wry expression on his face. "I can see by the way you look that my absence from my outfit was at the wrong time, unfortunately. Also, unfortunately, I trailed the horses alone. There's only my word for it."

But there was no hint of confession of guilt in his manner, no yielding to Alex's gaze. He was sure of his ability at taking care of himself in any move Alex made against him—almost vainly sure.

He spoke again. "Fact is, Briscoe, now that you say you were jumped by men dressed as Indians, it reminds me that I had the feelin' all along that it wasn't Indians who'd stampeded our stock either."

"How many of your horses did they get?"

"Four. All saddle stock."

"And all belonging to Shannon Southwestern, and branded, I take it?" Alex went on.

Capehart again eyed Alex carefully, knowing there was significance in that question. He answered thoughtfully. "Yes. We were bringin' 'em through from Santa Fe, along with a dozen loose harness horses. Now that you mention it, it seems odd that I got all the harness stuff back."

Alex said, "Yes." Capehart's story might explain how Shannon-branded horses had come into Bart Grassman's possession. Then again Capehart could have planned the stampede himself as a cover for joining Grassman and the other killers in ambushing the treasure wagons during his twenty-four hours' absence. Or at least planning the ambush with Grassman.

The doorbell sounded. Char, quick to seize a chance to interrupt the increasing tension between the two taut-faced men, went hurrying to answer.

She returned, ushering in Morgan Webb, the handsome man in evening dress whom Alex had seen earlier sitting at his desk in the office of Overland Transport.

Webb's wide brows arched. "Alex Briscoe!" he exclaimed. "You're home, safe! That's great! I was talking to Ellis Thayer only today, and he was worrying about you."

"I just pulled in," Alex explained.

"That's evident," Webb chuckled, his glance taking in Alex's appearance.

He nodded to Capehart, then crossed the room and took Char's hand. "A mighty becoming gown, Char," he said. "But it fails to do you justice, of course."

"There are some who differ with you," Char said.

25

Webb glanced at Alex and Capehart and laughed. "I see," he said. He was about forty, with powerfully hewn features. His dark, gray-flecked hair, which gave him a distinguished appearance, was brushed back from his forehead. He had started as swamper on wagon freighters as a boy and now owned his own company in the Santa Fe trade. Overland Transport was big and growing. And Webb had acquired polished manners and could take care of himself as a conversationalist. He was at home in his perfectly tailored evening dress.

He had a frank smile, and seemed the mildest of men, but Alex had seen him chastise tough, ham-handed bullwhackers in wagon-camp fights on two occasions in the past.

Morgan Webb had cut his opponents to pieces with fists that had been as wicked as clubs. He had delayed the knockouts for bloody minutes while he had piled on relentless punishment. There had been a merciless streak in him on those occasions.

Alex quietly studied Capehart and saw a little shadow of distaste for Webb in his eyes.

Webb, if he held the same aversion to the Tennessean, hid it under his affable manner. He glanced at his watch. "I would suggest that we head for the supper party," he said. "I brought a surrey."

He turned to Alex. "We freighting people are being entertained by none other than Jared Redfield in his private railway car," he explained. "Redfield, as you no doubt know, is one of the men who pull the financial strings in the East. He's here with other men on an inspection tour, and they have considerable to say about building the railroad. In fact, a nod of approval from Jared Redfield tonight will likely mean a fat contract for either Char or myself. We're competing with each other in bidding for a grading job. And I understand two army officers are to be at the supper to look us over also in regard to quartermaster freighting jobs."

He turned his engaging smile upon Char Shannon. "I'm afraid Jared Redfield will hardly notice me when Char is around in that dress," he smiled. "However, no matter who wins the job, Char and I will still be friends, just as we've always been. There are enough other opportunities for all of us. That's the theory on which Char's father and I operated, and that's the way Char and I will continue to operate, I hope. We . . ."

His voice trailed off. He was eying Char wonderingly.

"Char!" he exclaimed. "Is anything wrong? You're very pale. Are you ill?"

Char Shannon had not spoken a word all this time. She had been standing there, not seeing Morgan Webb at all. Alex realized that what she really had been looking at, eye to eye, was ruin, and the sight had not been attractive.

She aroused, forced herself to smile at Webb. "I'm all right, Morgan," she said. "I was just trying to work out a rather difficult business problem in my mind."

"Business," Webb scoffed. "Forget business, at least until after supper, Char."

Char turned to Alex. "I must see you again as soon as possible. This supper won't last more than a hour or two. Could you return here later? There are many things that need explaining."

She looked at him again. "But, of course, you must be very tired. How long has it been since you've slept?"

"I'll shave and find a tub of water," Alex said. "I'll come back and wait for you here."

He turned to leave the room. Capehart moved to his side and said, "It was horses I trailed, Briscoe, not wagons. Why would I try to ruin Char Shannon?"

"I accuse nobody—yet," Alex said. "Someday, however, I'll meet a certain man. I'll make him talk. Then I'll know the truth. If it's you, Len, I'll come after you myself. For the money was only the least of it. Three men were murdered, remember. They were friends of mine. They didn't deserve to die. Yes, I'll come after you."

"I'm sure you will," Capehart said, and stepped aside.

Alex walked out of the house, and Char Shannon followed him to the veranda and stood there, framed against the lamplight, thoughtfully watching him as he strode away.

He knew she was still there as he opened the gate and stepped out on the unpaved sidewalk.

Only then did he become aware that a man stood near the gate, just out of reach of the lamplight. The man evidently had been waiting purposely there, for he started to say something. Then that broke off in a gasp.

There was light enough from the open door and the windows of the house to reveal the shine of greasy, tangled hair and the shape of heavy, sloping shoulders. It was these characteristics that had enabled Alex to identify the man that night in the glow of the burning wagon on the Cimarron, even though he had worn a Kiowan feather and breechclout

27

and leggings, and had daubed his face and body with paint. Bart Grassman!

And with Grassman recognition was simultaneous. Alex believed the man had started to utter a name. He was certain Grassman had mistaken him for someone else as he emerged from Char Shannon's home.

But there was no mistake now. Whatever Grassman had intended to say was never uttered. He stood staring unbelievingly for a moment at Alex, whose body he had helped toss into the wagon with dead men many days ago.

He blurted out in a hoarse, choked voice, "Holy—holy! Briscoe! Alex Briscoe! You can't be . . ."

Then Bart Grassman went for his pistol with the frenzy of a man facing a fearful apparition that he must destroy.

Alex wanted Grassman alive, but he had no choice now. He drew and fired twice.

He felt the hot rush of the powder flame from Grassman's gun. Burning fragments bit into his face.

But the bullet missed, for Grassman, even as he had tripped the trigger, was pitching backwards. He fell on the packed earth of the sidewalk and twisted over on his side, his legs contorting in agony.

Alex saw that his bullets had torn through the man's chest. Grassman had only moments to live, for blood was spurting with each thrust of his heart.

Alex heard Char Shannon screaming, heard the pound of running feet approaching. Grassman writhed over on his back again, moaning faintly. Then the pain seemed to fade and he lay limp and spent.

Char Shannon came racing from the house bearing a lamp that had been burning on a stand in the hall. By its light Alex bent close over the dying man.

"Who put you up to it, Grassman?" he demanded, trying to force his will on the man's fading mind. "Who hired you to trail me from Santa Fe and ambush my wagons?"

Grassman's eyes rolled whitely. They were looking past Alex, as though trying to search out someone above him and behind him. "Comanch!" the man gasped. "They—they jumped us—next day after we—we got the—the bullion. I—I was lucky. Gone out to—to hunt meat. Saw—saw the fight—— All the others—killed—scalped."

"The bullion . . . ?" Alex said.

"Bullion—there on the plains," Grassman mumbled vaguely. "Boys cached it when—when they spotted—Indians. Tried to—to run fer it. Never—made it."

28

Then he was silent for a long time. "Comanch burned wagon," he said distinctly. "Bullion there—there not fur away."

That was the last Grassman ever was to speak.

Alex looked up. Len Capehart was standing above him, leaning close and listening intently.

Morgan Webb also gazed down at the dead man. With him was Char, horror and pity in her face. Webb had an arm around her as though to protect her from this ugly scene.

"Who is he, Alex?" Webb asked. "What was he trying to say? What was that you said to him? I didn't savvy."

Alex didn't answer. Sitting on his heels, he stared down at Bart Grassman's still face. The man's presence at the gate of the Shannon residence could not have been mere chance. Grassman was as travel-stained as Alex himself. It was evident he had just reached Hays and had hastened to the Shannon home to deliver a message to some particular person.

That message was that the treasue he and his men had stolen was still out there somewhere beyond the Jornada, near the ashes of another burned wagon and the charred bones of another group of men who had died in ambush.

Alex twisted around, looking up at Capehart, trying to read the man's expression in the lamplight. But Capehart's thin brown face was as inscrutable as ever.

Alex arose. A man who wanted to get in touch with Capehart in a hurry would probably go first to the Shannon residence to inquire his whereabouts. Alex felt that he was now sure of his quarry.

The shooting had attracted attention. Men were running from town. Alex saw Wild Bill Hickok's graceful figure riding toward the scene.

5 ★ AFTER ALEX had left her house, Amelia moved to the parlor and took her place primly in a straight chair, a sewing basket on the footstool beside her. She sat in the circle of lamplight, embroidery hoops in her lap and a bright silver thimble on her finger. Now and then she plied the needle, but such activity took place only when there were passers-by in the street. Mainly she sat rigid, thinking.

She knew she offered a chaste and winsome picture of

29

wifely diligence. The brass-bound Bible, the immaculate room, the warm pink light added to the effect. She had not drawn the curtains at this early hour. She often sat thus. She felt it was her duty to offer a reminder of refinement and rectitude to the inhabitants of this raw, boisterous boom town.

In contrast to this outer picture of contentment, within her raged a tumult of frustration. Whenever she let her glance turn to the windows, the lamplit palace car in which Jared Redfield was to entertain a supper party was plainly visible across open lots. She could see the bright glitter of the chandeliers.

Suddenly she arose and jerked the curtains savagely closed to shut out that sight. She barely restrained the desire to rip the curtains to shreds. She wanted to smash and destroy. She wanted to claw and rend. All the long-concealed hopes and ambitions and disappointments of her life closed in on her and took control of her.

News that Jared Redfield was to entertain at supper in his car had reached her the previous day from members of a sewing circle to which she belonged. It had aroused excited hope within her. To dine with Jared Redfield and his associates and their wives would be a distinct social triumph.

She was confident that, as a leader of culture in Hays City, she and her husband would be invited. She had been so sure of this she had stayed up the greater part of the previous night completing an evening dress. She had spent the morning working with hair curlers.

But, as the day had advanced, it had become evident that Jared Redfield was not aware of her existence. Worse yet, she had learned from a gossiping visitor that Charlotte Shannon was to be one of the supper guests.

Amelia had always been envious of Char Shannon. She had blamed her husband for this social slight. The tongue-lashing she had given Ellis had driven him back to his whiskey bottle, which lately had become his closest companion.

She was in this mood when another visitor knocked softly on the kitchen door. She stood a moment, debating whether to respond, for she knew the identity of this caller.

She moved through the hall into the kitchen, closing the intervening doors, and drew the curtains tighter. She opened the door. The arrival was Morgan Webb.

He entered, giving her his fine smile. "Good evening,

Amelia, my dear," he said in his sure and affable way. "I hope I'm not unwelcome."

He closed the door. Evidently he had come on foot across vacant lots. He wore a long dust coat and a wide-brimmed freighter's dark hat. It was apparent he had not wanted to be recognized on his way to this house.

Her heart leaped suddenly as he pulled off the duster and she saw that he was wearing evening dress.

"Oh, Morgan!" she exclaimed. "You're going to the Redfield supper! You came here to ask me. . . ."

Her voice drained off as she realized her eagerness had led her into jumping to a wrong conclusion. And it also placed her at a sudden disadvantage.

For Webb now studied her, his smile turning bold and knowing. As a casual business acquaintance of her husband he had been a visitor in their home only on rare occasions during the earlier months of their acquaintance.

Then, lately, he and her husband seemed to have suddenly developed many interests in common. This was not his first after-dark appearance at their kitchen door in recent days.

His attitude toward her in the past had been casually correct, but she knew he had always been fully aware she was a mature, desirable woman. And she also knew he had always been sure of his ability to sway her to his desires if he so willed. She had sensed this almost the first day of their meeting. She had held him at a distance, but had steeled herself to be prepared, for she had always known there would come a time when he would decide that such an association might be to his advantage. She was aware that this time had now arrived.

"I'm going to the supper, Amelia," he said. "But I'm escorting Char Shannon."

He saw that this angered her, and laughed. "Where's Ellis?" he asked.

She shrugged and gestured toward the upstairs.

"Drunk again?" Ugly impatience came into his voice.

"He was to have taken me to the supper," she said.

Webb knew that was an untruth. He laughed again, tolerantly. She fiercely resented the indifference with which he tore her pride away from her.

He saw this, and came suddenly, pulled her against him, and kissed her with the roughness of desire. He patted her familiarly. It was done with the air of a man who was foreclosing on a claim of which he was certain.

Amelia thrust her arm up the sleeve of his coat and raked her sharp, strong fingernails deeply into the flesh of his forearm.

Startled, stung, he swore in pain and pushed her ungently against the wall. "What was that for?" he demanded.

"You should thank me for being thoughtful," she said. "At least the mark won't show at the Redfield party. It might shock Char Shannon to know that you tried to make love to the wife of your friend."

The anger left Webb. He seemed pleased. "So that's why you bared your claws! Char Shannon!"

He kissed her again in a casual manner which left her infuriated. "With Char Shannon and me, it's purely a matter of business," he said. "At least tonight. But I wouldn't object, of course, to mixing pleasure with business, now that you've brought up the subject."

"You're vile," she said.

"You don't really believe that," he chuckled. He left her then, entered the hall, and mounted the stairs to the room where her husband lay.

Complete, tigerish fury possessed Amelia. She was a woman taunted. For the first time in her life she let herself give way to the desire to claw and kill. These impulses had struck her on occasions in the past, but she had always mastered them.

She walked into the parlor, seized up a pistol from a drawer in the writing desk where Ellis always kept a loaded weapon. She mounted three or four steps of the stairway with the softness of a stalking cat.

Then reason prevailed. She paused, and the fury cooled. She began thinking precisely again. She could hear Webb and her husband talking in murmurs. She strained to listen, but was able to make out only that Webb was angry over Ellis's drinking and was warning him to pull himself together and stay away from the bottle.

There was something completely abject and groveling in her husband's fervent promises that he would comply. This was not the first time Webb and Ellis had conferred in whispers just beyond reach of her ears.

These conferences had started after Webb had returned from a fast and mysterious trip to Santa Fe. It was after these talks had begun that Ellis had surprised her by announcing that he was selling his partnership in Alex Briscoe's company.

At first Amelia had opposed selling a profitable investment,

32

and particularly to Char Shannon. But something in Ellis's demeanor had silenced her.

She had never been able to catch more than a few disconnected words during her eavesdropping, but she had heard Alex's name mentioned more than once. And she had watched Ellis start drinking and had seen the signs of dissolution grow in him, as though his conscience were torturing him.

Alex's revelation that murder and a wagonload of treasure were involved had given her the answer to the reason for Webb's hushed visits.

She knew now why that hunted look had grown in her husband's eyes, and why he had taken to drinking alone and cowering in his room the greater part of the time.

Ellis Thayer had taken blood money. He had profited because of advance knowledge that a robbery was to be perpetrated. Then, when he realized that murder had also been committed, his character had not been able to stand up under such a responsibility.

Webb now descended the stairs. He was flushed and angry. "Fill him with black coffee, Amelia!" he commanded peremptorily. "Sober him, and keep him cooped up here."

He added wrathfully, "The sot! The weakling!"

He patted her again, giving her his knowing smile, and departed by the way he had come. Presently she heard his surrey, which he had left at a distance, move away, the sounds receding in the direction of the Shannon residence.

She returned to the parlor and to her sewing basket. She picked up the needle. With furious deliberation she pressed the point down onto the marble stand, jamming it with the thimble in the outbursting rage of a demeaned woman.

The needle snapped. "Damn him!" she breathed chokingly. "Damn Alex Briscoe! Damn Char Shannon! Damn them all!"

She sat there then for a long time, her bloodless fingers locked tight in her lap, staring straight ahead at nothing. She was replanning her life.

Presently Ellis came hesitantly down the stairs and gazed at her with apprehension. He wore his coat and hat and carried his walking cane, which was one of his emblems of importance.

"Going for some fresh air," he said uncertainly.

Amelia made no attempt to halt him. For something more potent than coffee had sobered him. She looked at him without speaking. Panic came into his bloodshot eyes. He hurried past her and out of the house—a man shrunken by the realization of her knowledge of him and her determination to use it as a weapon against him.

Amelia continued to sit motionless. The sharp crash of gunshots startled her. Three overlapping reports. They came from the direction of the Shannon home a block away.

She sprang to her feet. "Alex!" she breathed. "He—he and Len Capehart . . . !"

Windows and doors banged open in the town. Men began hurrying in the street. She heard boys running and shouting to each other. She stepped out of the house and walked to the gate.

A rider passed by at a trot presently, and she made out the erect figure and long hair and sweeping mustache of Wild Bill Hickok, the town marshal.

"What is it, Marshal?" she called.

"A shootin' of some kind, seems like, ma'am," Hickok explained over his shoulder as he trotted his horse onward.

The trouble seemed to be at the Shannon home. Amelia could see a crowd gathering there.

She ran to the house, tied a scarf over her hair, then hurried down the dark, dusty street toward the center of the excitement. It was not exactly proper for a woman of virtue to be alone at this hour, but she had to know what had happened.

Hickok's big figure loomed in the midst of the bystanders. He was talking to Alex. Char Shannon was in the circle also, wearing a smart evening gown. She was holding a lamp which illuminated the group. This she placed on the ground. Len Capehart stood there also.

Then Amelia's glance rested on Morgan Webb, who stood close at Char's side. She saw that a man's body was lying on the sidewalk at Hickok's feet. Someone who had been bending over the outstretched figure straightened. It was Will Lewis, the doctor.

"Dead!" Will Lewis said. "Bullets in the lungs."

Hickok turned to Char Shannon. He removed his hat. "You heard what Alex Briscoe said, Miss Shannon," he said. "He stated that this man, Bart Grassman, seemed to be waiting for him here on the sidewalk as he came from your house, and that Grassman went for his gun first. Were you in a position to see what happened?"

"Yes," Char Shannon said. "I saw it all."

"Do you want to tell me now, or would you prefer to wait until you testify at the inquest tomorrow?" Hickok asked.

34

"It happened exactly as Mr. Briscoe described it," Char Shannon said. "I was standing in the door, and the light reached them. Grassman seemed startled when he recognized Mr. Briscoe. Then he snatched out his gun. But——"

Her gaze drifted broodingly to Alex. "Mr. Briscoe drew and fired twice so fast I couldn't believe it," she went on. "Grassman's gun exploded too, but an instant later. Then he fell."

"Thank you kindly, Miss Shannon," Hickok said. "You'll repeat that under oath, I take it?"

"Certainly," Char said.

"Stay in town for the inquest, Alex," Hickok said. "Do you know why Grassman went for his pistol when he saw you?"

"Grassman made a mistake," Alex commented. "He acted like he was seeing a ghost."

"He did make a mistake," Hickok said dryly. "His last one. You're not even allowed one error in that kind of a game."

6 ★ ALEX LOOKED at Char Shannon and said, "Thanks!"

She did not answer. She linked arms with Morgan Webb and Capehart and started toward the house.

Abruptly she turned and walked back to speak to Alex alone. "Apparently you forgot one detail when you told us how you escaped alive from that ambush," she murmured. "You failed to mention that you had recognized Bart Grassman as one of the killers that night."

Alex said nothing, waiting her next move.

"You didn't mention it to Hickok either," she went on. "Grassman worked as a teamster for us. In fact, my father hired him personally to handle a Shannon wagon on the spring trip to Santa Fe."

"Why are you telling me this?" Alex asked.

"You know why. You believe Grassman came to this house tonight to find Len Capehart. You believe that because Grassman and Len both were in Santa Fe that Len engineered what happened to you on the trail. You must have other reasons for that belief. What are they?"

"Let's just say that I have other reasons," Alex said, his unshaven face hard and unyielding.

Char Shannon's eyes moved to the pistol that hung at his side. The tang of powder smoke was still strong in the air.

She suddenly shuddered. "Don't—don't jump to the wrong conclusion!" she breathed imploringly. "Len is not—cannot be a—a murderer. It would be a terrible thing, a tragic mistake if you—if you went gunning for each other."

She turned away then. But once more she was halted. A man wearing evening dress under a linen dust coat alighted from a rented hansom cab that had just pulled up. He called, "Miss Shannon! Just a moment, please!"

Char returned at a run, holding her skirts above her high-heeled slippers. The arrival was a big, vigorous elderly man with graying bushy hair and sideburns.

"Oh, Mr. Redfield!" she exclaimed apologetically. "I'm sorry we've been delayed. I hope we haven't ruined your supper party. We——"

"Apologies are unnecessary, of course, my dear," the gray-haired man said. "I understand there was some kind of a pistol duel."

"Mr. Redfield, this is Alex Briscoe, in whose freighting company I bought a partnership recently. Mr. Briscoe was involved in the duel, but escaped injury. The—the other man was—was killed."

Jared Redfield peered at Alex, then extended a hand. "I knew your father well, Briscoe," he said. "Evidently you have inherited his fighting ability, and his speed with a gun. I was a wagon freighter myself in my younger years. I was well acquainted with Char's father also in those days. In fact, Tom Briscoe and Barney Shannon and I were all close friends until——"

He broke off, as though realizing he was saying too much. He glanced uneasily at Char and changed the subject. "Supper is still waiting, of course," he said. "I'd be happy, Briscoe, if you would accept a belated invitation to join us."

Alex shrugged. "In addition to not being dressed for a festive occasion, you can understand that I'm surely not in the mood, after what happened. I don't engage in gun fights every day, no matter what impression you may have of me."

"I understand," Redfield said. "But this is not really a festive matter. It is business rather than pleasure, and I would consider it a favor if you could stretch a point by joining us. Appearances don't count under the circumstances."

A figure stepped from the darkness behind them, and Alex felt an eager hand close on his arm. It was Amelia, a scarf tied around her hair.

"Alex!" she breathed excitedly, her eyes big and pleading. "After all, you can shave! And you do have other clothes."

36

Amelia looked shyly at Jared Redfield, her eyes dropping in confusion. "Please forgive me for being so forward, Mr. Redfield," she stammered. "But I was bold enough to walk past your railway car early this evening and peek. It would be just—just heavenly to sit at a civilized table again. We so rarely have such opportunity here in this wild town. Alex doesn't know what he is passing up to refuse such an evening."

Alex smiled. "This is Mrs. Ellis Thayer. She is the wife of my former partner."

Jared Redfield bowed and chuckled. "I insist, Mrs. Thayer, that you also honor us with your presence. I know Briscoe can't refuse now that I have your help in persuading him. I trust that you will find us as civilized as you hope."

"Thank you!" Amelia said happily.

Alex felt her fingers tighten demandingly on his arm. He did not have the heart to disappoint her. "Could we have thirty minutes or so?" he asked Redfield.

"An hour at least," Amelia said hastily.

"And longer if you wish, my dear," Redfield smiled.

Alex was aware of a triumph in Amelia as he escorted her to her home. He then rode across town to the home of Hoxie and Julia Carver, with whom he boarded. Hoxie, yard boss at Alex's headquarters, had been with Briscoe & Company for years. He sat listening, his seamed face grim, while Alex talked as he shaved, bathed, and dressed.

Alex told what had happened to the treasure wagons and of his gun fight with Grassman. He avoided mentioning his belief that Len Capehart had been the instigator of the ambush. He wanted to see what conclusion Hoxie would draw from the facts.

"Did anybody but yourself hear what Grassman told you before he died?" Hoxie asked.

"I'm sure Capehart did. But that won't do anyone much good. I'm the only person who knows where my wagons were ambushed in the first place."

"Anybody else?" Hoxie asked.

"Char Shannon, perhaps. Morgan Webb was there also and might have been close enough to have heard."

"Morg, huh?" Hoxie sniffed. "Seems like he generally is around. He's just about got a clear road to eatin' high on the hawg in the freightin' business from now on."

Alex frowned absently. Morgan Webb had been furthest from his thoughts.

Hoxie puffed his clay pipe. "Now that you're done for, an'

draggin' Char Shannon down with you, Morg will be a mighty big frog in a mighty big pond," he went on. "Why, he's the only freighter strong enough now to step in an' take over the business o' Briscoe & Company an' Shannon Southwestern."

He watched the frown grow on Alex's brow. "You don't believe me," he snorted. "You've been so cussed busy tryin' to bid business away from Shannon Southwestern, just like yore paw did before you, that you missed the way Morg has been pickin' ripe plums while you an' Barney Shannon fought over green persimmons. Morg started out in the Santa Fe trade with one patched wagon an' four yoke of bony oxen. That's the way you an' others still think o' him. But Morg, right now, owns almost as much stock an' wheels as either you or Charlotte Shannon. An' he'll have all these railroad an' army contracts thet are hangin' ripe an' juicy on the trees."

"What are you trying to say, Hoxie?"

"Ain't tryin'. I'm sayin'. Morg Webb talks like he feeds on soft soap. He's fooled most folks, but I happen to know there's hard formation under that toothy smile o' his. He rode with Quantrill's guerrillas durin' the war. Under another name, o' course."

"I've heard talk along that line," Alex said slowly. "Are you sure?"

"I'm sure." Hoxie nodded. "An', if you ask me, Morg never changed his spots. He's still guerrilla. He's gettin' rich. He even struts when he rides by on them Kentucky horses thet he's breedin'. An' he's importin' gunmen. Old pals, I reckon. Most of 'em likely rode guerrilla too, or I don't know how to read sign."

"Gunmen? Importing them? Why?"

"Maybe to see thet his wagon an' stable crews earn their pay," Hoxie growled. "Maybe to see thet shippers pay whatever rate Morg wants to charge after he monopolizes the Santa Fe trade. What do most men hire gunmen for? To ride with sharp spurs over other folks, thet's why. An' Keno Dane is here as ramrod of his shooters."

"Keno Dane? The Texas killer?"

"Dane's been on Morg's payroll more'n a month now." Hoxie nodded. "I saw him only tonight at Morg's yards wearin' that pair of big pearl-handled .44's that he must sleep with."

Alex recalled the man he had seen in Webb's office. "I saw him too. But I didn't know who he was."

"Let's hope you never git better acquainted with him,"

38

Hoxie said. "You took good care of yourself agin Bart Grassman tonight, but Dane comes tougher. He's killed maybe half dozen men."

Alex ran a comb through his thick hair. "I need shearing around the ears," he said, and went to the living room, where Julia Carver, a plump, kindly woman, was knitting, and cajoled her into trimming his hair back from his ears and collar.

"You need sleep instead o' stayin' up to all hours of the night, drinkin' an' carryin' on with millionaires and girls like Char Shannon," Julia told him severely.

"I've got some questions to ask Jared Redfield," Alex said. "He started to tell me how he and Dad and Barney Shannon had been close friends when they were young men until something happened. At that point he closed up as tight as a bullfrog full of buckshot. I've always wanted to know what started that grudge."

Hoxie and his wife looked at each other, but said nothing.

A hostler, on Hoxie's order, had brought a top buggy and a smart team of sorrels up from the stables. Hoxie walked with Alex to the rig.

"Tomorrow have a wagon worked over and shaped up for a fast, hard trip," Alex said. "Pick out the best twelve-footer in the yards. That's big enough, without being too heavy. I want to move fast. I'll need a six hitch and two, maybe three, spares. Duns and grays. Those colors aren't easily seen at a distance on the plains. Fit the wagon with old, weathered canvas. I want horses fresh and grained that can knock off the miles under pressure. I'll pick out a good man tomorrow to go with me. Shorty McVey, if he's in off the road. He's tough, loyal, and can shoot. We'll need four rifles and a couple thousand rounds of——"

"Sounds like you might be aimin' to go back across the Jornada."

"I'm starting tomorrow night." Alex nodded. "Don't let anyone know you're outfitting the wagon. Pick a couple of good men and let them take care of it under cover in one of the barns. I can cut the trail at the point on the Cimarron where Grassman's outfit dry-gulched us, and ought to be able to locate where they cached the bullion when the Comanches hit them."

Hoxie shook his head. "Two men with a wagon might be lucky enough to cross that stretch to the Cimarron alive, but it'd be nigh a miracle," he said. "It'd be two miracles if they got back safe. You don't savvy how fast this Indian war has

39

spread. Every tribe from the Platte to the Mex border is on the prod. For once, the Indians are standin' together instead o' fightin' each other."

"You forget——"

"Yeah, I know. You an' Bart Grassman come out o' the Jornada alive just lately. An' Capehart got through with four wagons. There's been a few others that's made it, I reckon. Fools for luck, all o' you. Because there's others that have tried it an' air still out there. Plenty of 'em. Coyotes an' magpies have took care o' what's left of 'em. Even the long trail past Bent's old fort an' Dick Wootton's toll road at Raton Pass ain't bein' traveled this summer. The tribes air ridin' even north o' the Arkansas."

"There's no other way," Alex said.

"There's a safer way. A lot of freighters aim to make a try. We got together lately, for we've got a lot of valuable freight for the Southwest thet ought to go through before winter. Fifty wagons with an extra man in each crew have already been signed up. We'll be strong enough so the Indians will think twice before jumpin' us. The string pulls out the day after tomorrow, if everybody can get ready. I'm sendin' two o' your Briscoe wagons. Char Shannon will have two or three also, an' I hear Morg Webb is sendin' at least four. There's about twenty immigrants, bound fer Arizona, who've been waitin' to go through, who'll be in line also."

He let Alex think that over. "What you ought to do is travel acrost the Jornada with this big string," he went on. "Take two, three good men with you, an' when you reach the place near where you want to start yore hunt you kin part company with the string. With a good team an' wagon you'd then have a better chance o' makin' it back to Fort Dodge, for you'd have mounts fairly fresh an' you'd be able to travel fast at night."

Alex stood frowning, rebelling at the thought of delay. Travel with a big wagon train means slow progress.

It had been scarcely an hour since Grassman's dying words had revived in him the flaming hope that he might recover the bullion intact. Grassman evidently had been certain that the Comanches had not been aware of the presence of the cached treasure when they burned the wagon.

The man had also said that the Indian attack had come the day after the treasure had fallen into his hands. That might or might not be accurate. In any event, at least twenty-four hours must have elapsed after he and his men had left

40

Alex for dead. They could have made two marches in that time, and might have traveled up to sixty miles or more—and in an unknown direction.

Alex's hopes sank as he comprehended the enormity of his task. In that rolling, broken country, baking under the August sun, with its shimmering distances and its barren, yellow bluffs, dry streams, and drifting buffalo herds, a heap of ashes would be a mere speck.

However, he had one advantage. He was sure he would have no difficulty finding the spot where he had escaped from the other burning wagon. From that point he hoped to be able to trace the heavily laden vehicle that had been driven away.

But that might take days—even weeks, if the trail had been wind-blown or thunderstorms had swept the plains. And it might be utterly impossible. The bond Alex had signed at Santa Fe was subject to forfeit if the shipment of treasure was not delivered to its destination within sixty days. However, he knew the consignees in Santa Fe would waive such a formality if the bullion could be recovered. Even so, time was against him, and each day's delay brought him and Char Shannon that nearer to disaster.

He stood harassed, thinking over Hoxie's advice. "I still figure I must make the try, and should start tomorrow night," he said.

He stepped into the carriage and drove to Amelia's house. It was Ellis who admitted him. Alex was shocked. At first he could not believe that the unkempt, unshaven man with the wild, bloodshot eyes was really the same fastidious Ellis Thayer who had been his partner.

"If you've come here to upbraid me for selling out to Charlotte Shannon you're wasting your time, Alex," Ellis began with the rushing breathlessness of a man who was forcing himself to face an issue. "I saw my chance to make a good and honest profit and would have been a fool to have turned it down. You'd have done the same if you'd been in my situation."

Alex saw that Ellis was drunk. That astonished him also, for Ellis had always been a very moderate drinker.

"It's done and can't be undone, Ellis," he said. "And you were a lot luckier than you realized. You sold at the right time. Has Amelia told you what happened to me on the trail?"

"She told me! She told me!" Ellis's voice rose. "Are you implying that I knew——?"

Amelia came hurrying into the room. "Ellis! Ellis!" she cried. "Calm down!"

She stroked his face soothingly. "Now, now!" she crooned. "Alex doesn't hold any anger toward you, dear. Quit blaming yourself."

Ellis suddenly buried his face in his hands and began sobbing. Alex stood appalled. Amelia gave him a tragic look, then led her husband from the room and upstairs.

It was some minutes before she returned. She daubed away tears. "He's asleep, thank heaven," she sighed. "I feel so ashamed about—about everything. And above all, about the drinking. He's been worrying about what you may think of him, and has turned to drink to ease his conscience. My husband feels that he let you down. It only made it worse when I told him about the loss of the bullion. But—let's not talk about it tonight, Alex. Let's forget our troubles and enjoy ourselves for a few hours at least."

Amelia wore an evening gown in a warm shade of gray. It was modestly revealing of shoulder and bosom. Her hair was done in a new style. She was more than comely. She was an alluring, seductive woman.

She watched Alex's expression and laughed guiltily. "Thank you," she murmured.

"For what?"

"For complimenting my attire by disapproving of it," she smiled. "I know it's a trifle daring, but I feel now that I can really compete with Char Shannon on equal terms. Your scowl is good for my self-esteem."

7 ★ JARED REDFIELD'S long-delayed supper was still waiting, along with his guests, when Alex and Amelia were ushered into the elegant palace car.

There were half a dozen other freighting men or town businessmen and their wives, whom they knew. Redfield introduced them to three middle-aged men and their wives. These were financial men, associated with Redfield and the railroad. An army general and a colonel from the quartermaster department were engaged in a lively conversation with Char Shannon. Len Capehart stood in the background, smoking a brown paper cigarette. Morgan Webb was expansively jovial as he chatted with the financial man.

A waiter brought champagne, but Amelia refused. "I never touch intoxicating beverages," she said stiffly.

She shook hands with Char. "Your gown," she said, "is lovely. You make me feel rather old-fashioned in this dress."

Char produced a cigarette case, snapped it open, and offered it to Amelia.

She recoiled. "Oh my, no!" she exclaimed. "I wouldn't think of such a thing."

Char calmly helped herself to one of the cigarettes. There was an uncomfortable moment, and then Jared Redfield moved hastily to strike a match and offer it.

Apparently oblivious of the shocked expressions of the staring women guests and the dazed fascination of their husbands, Char blew a thin streamer of smoke. "Surely, Mrs. Thayer," she said, "you must have some little vice or other? Perhaps you use opium?"

Amelia chose to ignore that. Even Morgan Webb had stopped talking for a moment while he gazed reprovingly. Capehart stonily eyed the nonchalant Char.

It was a stiff and awkward supper. Alex regretted now that he had come here. It had been a mistake. It was his presence that laid a damper on the group. He had killed a man this same evening, and he saw the shine of morbid curiosity in the eyes of the men, and also in the women. Particularly in the women.

He began to shrink and sweat. He became acutely conscious of their covert stares.

"They must think I'm a cold-blooded fish," he murmured to Amelia. "A monster, coming here to a champagne party and listening to gay talk after what happened."

"Now don't do anything to spoil my evening," Amelia protested anxiously. "Let them stare. Why, you've become a celebrity, Alex."

"A celebrity? Because I was forced to kill a man?"

"Be quiet!" she breathed, an impatient temper in her. She added accusingly, "You must be drinking too much."

As a matter of fact, Alex had not touched the champagne glass at his plate. A celebrity! What Amelia really had meant was that he was now looked upon as a killer. Like Hickok, like Len Capehart, he was now bearing that same whispered label.

For the first time he had a chance to think clearly. He went over again in his mind that moment when he had stepped through the gate at Char Shannon's home to face a man who had tried to shoot him.

His own reaction had been instinctive. He had drawn and fired with no conscious thought except that of self-preservation. Until now that shooting had hardly seemed real. It was as though someone else had killed Bart Grassman.

Now the aftermath struck at his nerves. He found his palms moist and cold. Dampness broke out on his forehead.

He discovered that Char Shannon, who was sitting opposite him, was watching him. She leaned across the table. "What happened tonight wasn't your fault," she murmured. "Don't let these people glare you down."

That strengthened him and carried him through the supper.

Amelia was oblivious of his ordeal. She was seated at Jared Redfield's right, although that position of prestige had been intended for the wife of one of the financiers. Amelia had occupied it under an apparent misunderstanding. She chatted animatedly with Redfield, who appeared slightly bewildered by the attention of so attractive a female.

When coffee was finally served, Redfield arose. "Ladies," he said, "we must beg you to excuse us for a little while. We have a business matter, and the discussion would only bore you. Come, gentlemen. And you also, Miss Shannon, if you will."

Redfield led the way to the rear of the car, where a space had been fitted to serve as an office. He drew a curtain across the car, giving privacy to this area. He seated Char and motioned the others to chairs.

"I'll come to the point," he said. "Our purpose in visiting Hays City is to view construction and to arrange financing of further grading westward. It is the grading contract that we are to consider this evening."

He looked around. "Several bids have been made by various firms, but the majority were not responsible, or lack the necessary equipment and financial reserves. Therefore we have seriously considered only the offers made by Miss Shannon in behalf of Shannon Southwestern and by Morgan Webb for his Overland Transport."

He studied the tip of his cigar a moment before proceeding. "I'll be frank, gentlemen," he said. "I had dealings with both Barney Shannon and Tom Briscoe in the past. When I learned that the companies they founded were to be combined I made up my mind to recommend that the terms proposed by Miss Shannon be accepted. I felt that the organizations they had built up would be more than sufficient to

44

carry out the work, and I am certain that both Miss Char, the daughter of one, and Alex, the son of the other, would be as faithful in the performance of the contract as their fathers would have been. In other words, I have confidence in them."

He turned to Morgan Webb. "I do not intend that as a reflection on you, Mr. Webb. It is merely a case of doing business with organizations I have dealt with before. However, in addition, the Shannon bid was considerably under your figures."

Webb swallowed hard. The muscles bunched along his jaws and disappointment drove angry color into his face. He fought all of this down and shrugged. "If I'm licked, I'm licked. Congratulations, Char."

Jared Redfield shook his head. "That may be a trifle premature, I'm afraid. The situation has changed considerably in the past hour. Miss Shannon has informed me privately that certain events have taken place that might make it impossible for the Shannon, Briscoe company to fulfill the contract."

"What!" Webb exclaimed. "Char! What's happened?"

"Plenty," Char said.

"Because of this," Redfield went on reluctantly, "I can see no alternative other than to accept Mr. Webb's——"

Alex interrupted him. "Briscoe & Shannon requests that any decision in the matter be delayed."

Redfield brightened. "That might be possible," he said hopefully. "For how long?"

"Sixty days," Alex said after a moment of calculation.

"Sixty days!" Webb almost yelled. "That would not be fair, Mr. Redfield. I came here tonight prepared to sign a contract at once."

He turned to Char. "What's this all about, my dear?"

Char answered frankly. "Alex Briscoe brought me some very bad news tonight. He had been held up during the trip from Santa Fe by a gang of men dressed as Indians. A considerable shipment of gold and silver bullion that he was moving under bond from Santa Fe to Hays City was stolen. As his partner I am liable for the loss also."

"Jupiter!" Webb gasped. "Alex! Where did all this happen?"

"It happened," Alex said.

"I'm sorry, Char," Webb said. "Sincerely sorry. I don't like profiting by other's misfortunes. Still, it is part of the business. We all take our risks. Mr. Redfield, I feel that it would be unjust to my company to put off this decision. What purpose would it serve to stall around?"

Redfield ignored his advisers, who were nodding their heads in obvious agreement with Webb. "Have you any reason to offer for seeking a delay, Alex?" he asked.

"The best," Alex said. "I expect before the time expires to have the bullion back in our possession."

"You mean you figure you can run down these trail robbers?" Webb asked skeptically. "That's a pretty long gamble. Or maybe you have something definite to work on?"

"Maybe," Alex said.

Webb shrugged, glanced significantly at Redfield's group, and said, "I insist that this farfetched request be——"

"As long as the work can't start until spring anyway, there could be no harm in putting off the matter for a few weeks," Alex interrupted.

Jared Redfield studied Alex a moment. Then Char. "Sixty days it is," he said crisply. "But not a minute more. Not a second. It is only fair that we give Miss Shannon and Briscoe a chance to solve their financial difficulties, gentlemen. Now, is there anything else to discuss? If not, let us return to the ladies."

The gathering broke up. Jared Redfield had used his power of leadership to override majority opinion in favor of his own personal judgment. Morgan Webb stalked into the main car and barked at a waiter, ordering whiskey.

Alex found Char eying him thoughtfully. On an impulse he offered her his arm. He expected her to ignore him in favor of Len Capehart, who was waiting, but she placed her fingertips on his sleeve and walked with him through the car. This nearness, suddenly, was disconcerting to him. More than before he became acutely aware that she was a gorgeous creature.

"We have Redfield on our side at least," he murmured.

"I could hug him," she said. "And I will at first chance. It was like having a lifeline hit you when you were drowning. Apparently we have the memory of our respective fathers to thank for this. Mr. Redfield seemed to have a lot of respect for them." She added, after a moment of hesitation, "Both of them."

"And he seems to know some things about them better than I do," Alex said. He was thinking of the feud that had parted his father and Barney Shannon.

"Do you really think you can find the bullion?"

46

"We'll know one way or another before the sixty days are up," he said. "I'll talk to the banks tomorrow. The bullion was consigned to them. They'll go along with me, I'm sure, for it will be to their benefit, and to the shippers' back in Santa Fe as well, if I can get the stuff back. You heard what Grassman said before he died, I believe. I intend to pull out tomorrow night with a fast team and a wagon."

"For the Jornada? Alone?"

"I'll take another man, if I can find one I trust. But two is the limit for fast travel and for keeping under cover."

"It will be terribly dangerous," she said. "Too dangerous. There's a better way. A combined train of fifty wagons or more is moving out the day after tomorrow to——"

"I know," Alex shrugged. "But time is precious. I can travel faster than——"

"A few days, more or less, hardly matters now. It will lessen the danger if you travel with the big string at least part of the day."

She paused, then added slowly, "You must realize that if anything happens to you there is little chance the bullion will ever be found—at least in time to save Briscoe & Shannon. You're the only one who knows the starting point in the search."

Alex sat scowling, frustrated. She had him pinned down by logic. Finally he shrugged. "You're right, I'm afraid," he said. "I'll crawl along with them at least until we get near the Cimarron."

"I have the other man you need," she said.

When he turned quickly to stare at her, she added, "Len Capehart."

Before he could speak, she silenced him. "I know you believe Len was back of what happened to you. Just what your evidence is, you've never said. But I'm sure you're wrong. Len is going with you as my representative."

"You two seemed to have decided this beforehand."

"We talked it over a little while ago," she said calmly. "We both heard what Grassman said to you. And, knowing how stubborn and self-sufficient you are, I was sure you would set off alone and try to find the treasure."

She added casually, "I'm going with the big string also."

"You?"

"I may even go along to hunt for the bullion," she said. "That remains to be seen. If the Indian trouble has died down, and it is reasonably safe, I will stay with you and Len. We're not needed here right now. Hoxie Carver, your yard boss, and Bill Weaver at my father's—at our yards can handle the barns until we get back. They've been in charge many times before. It would be as well if I go on to Santa Fe anyway. One of us will have to go there sooner or later to arrange for consolidating our yards."

"First, you've got to know whether there's anything left to consolidate." Alex shrugged. "What you really mean is that you aim to go along to make sure I don't try to run a sandy on you."

"Perhaps," she said coolly.

"The trail is no place for a woman," he said.

She uttered a sniff of scorn. "Bosh! I first traveled down to Santa Fe with a bull train when I was a child. I've heard the Cheyenne war whoop. And I've heard the Pawnee whistle. I've seen Apaches on the sky line. I can handle stock—mules, horses, or oxen. And I know which end of a rifle the bullets come out of."

Jared Redfield joined them at that moment, escaping from Amelia, who had kept him buttonholed. He held a brandy glass and rolled its contents meditatively.

"I'm happy you frankly told me your financial problem, Charlotte," he said. "Some persons seeking a contract would have kept your situation secret, hoping to make out by hook or crook. That was why I so quickly favored giving you and Alex the chance to work out your problem. I have been wondering all day which course you would select. And you picked the right one. I thought you would."

"All day?" Alex questioned quickly.

"I thought that statement would surprise you," Redfield said. "As I understood your story, Charlotte, you were not aware of the situation that had overtaken Alex until he arrived at your home this evening. But someone else in town apparently had the information before that. Read this."

He produced a square of cheap writing paper. Penciled in letters that were roughly blocked out in order to disguise the handwriting was this message:

Redfield:
Char Shannon is about bankrupt. Don't deal with her. She'll never make good on any contract the railroad gives her.

A Friend

"Where did this come from?" Alex asked tersely.

"Someone pushed it beneath the door of the car sometime last night," Redfield said. "It was found by the porter this morning."

"Last night!" Char exclaimed. Her gaze swung abruptly to Alex. And there it was again—the doubt and the uncertainty.

"I was miles away, riding the trail from Fort Dodge last night," he said. "Does that answer your question?"

"I asked no question," she said.

"But you're not entirely sure, are you?" he snapped. "Nor about where I was the night of the fire."

"Apparently someone who had knowledge of the ambush preceded both you and this man Grassman to Hays City," Redfield commented.

Alex said nothing. He felt there was one positive answer to the question as to that person's identity. Len Capehart had been in Hays several days since his return from Santa Fe.

But there were other questions not as easy to answer. Why would Capehart send that note to Jared Redfield? At best it seemed to be an unnecessary risk. At worst it was a calculated blow at Char Shannon, for that message was designed to speed her company toward ruin.

His glance picked out Capehart, who stood alone, a glass in his hand from which he sipped meditatively. The Tennessean did not seem to be watching anyone, particularly Char. Despite that, he was watching her, Alex realized, and with a deep and longing interest.

The champagne was having its effect upon some of the guests. The talk and the laughter had moved to a higher pitch, creating a din in the confined space that began to grind on Alex's nerves. He was aware of his weariness.

Char and Redfield were still looking at him, expecting him to make some reply to the last remark. He was spared that.

With violent impact a six-shooter bellowed in the darkness outside the car. The glass in a window shattered and fragments showered the interior. The gun exploded again, the spurt of flame leaping through the opening. A window on the opposite of the car was smashed by this second bullet.

Alex hurled himself forward and his shoulder crashed into Char, driving her to the floor and out of the line of further slugs. "Are you hurt?" he snapped.

"No!" she gasped. "No—no!"

He leaped to his feet, ran to the forward door of the car, and snatched it open. He heard Capehart at his heels as he reached the platform.

They dropped to the ground together. Morgan Webb, a pistol in his hand, came racing out of the darkness to join them. Evidently he had alighted from the opposite end of the car.

They stood, holding their breath, listening, but some of the women in the parlor car were screaming hysterically. A yard engine came booming down the line. These interruptions drowned out any sounds the assassin might have been making in his retreat, Alex decided.

Directly before them were sidings on which stood strings of boxcars and flats. In the opposite direction loomed the shape of the gable-roofed depot, which was closed and unlighted at this hour. Beyond were more sidings and cattle chutes and a clutter of warehouses and wagon yards.

They spread out in various directions. Alex searched among railway sidings until he realized it was a waste of time. He returned and met Capehart, who also had given up the hunt. Webb was more persistent, but he finally came striding back, shrugging in defeat.

They climbed into the car. Some of the women were still hysterical. Char was trying to soothe them. Amelia was moving about helplessly, clasping and unclasping hands, and staring in horror at the bullet-shattered windows.

Alex and Jared Redfield walked to these windows and studied them, trying to make out the angle at which the bullets had been fired.

"Who in the world could they have been aimed at?" Redfield said.

Len Capehart spoke. "Couldn't rightly say who he was notchin' in his sight, but he must have come within peach fuzz of gettin' either you, or Char or Briscoe. The two hunks of lead must have passed right between the three of you."

Alex was looking at Char. He moved suddenly to her and pushed back her dark hair. A small strand of it came loose in his grasp. It had been severed by a bullet. Just below the tip of her left ear was a small red welt from which blood was oozing.

"He didn't miss entirely," he said.

A strangled, gasping sound came. Amelia Thayer clutched dizzily at the back of a chair, then sank suddenly into it. She lapsed into a dead faint, her head sagging back limply.

Morgan Webb brought water and helped Char revive her. Presently she sat up weakly. But the horror was still in her. And there was something else in her eyes that Alex could not define.

All the excitement had sustained Char until now. Alex brought a dampened napkin and said, "Hold this on that bullet burn a moment."

She abruptly went as pale as chalk and swayed a little. He grasped her by the arms and shook her gently. He saw the faintness pass.

"Why—why would anyone want to kill me?" she asked shakily.

There was no answer to that.

8 ★ AMELIA REMAINED wanly in the chair in the parlor car for a time. Finally she told Alex she felt up to going home. He helped her from the car and to the carriage.

The party was breaking up. Char was being handed into Webb's surrey by Jared Redfield. Capehart wedged his long legs in the back seat as Webb freed the reins from the whipstock.

"Excuse me a moment, Amelia," Alex said.

He walked to the surrey. "I hear you're pulling out with a big string, Len," he said to Capehart. "You and Miss Shannon. I'm making the trip also. I hope you don't change your mind?"

"Nor you, Briscoe," Capehart said. "I'm countin' on your company."

Webb spoke in his cheery voice. "Well, now, that's pleasant news. Char, you didn't tell me you were going down to Santa Fe with us. That'll shorten the miles. It happens that I'm traveling with my wagons also. I'm sending three or four, depending on how much payload we have on the warehouse floor. I've got considerable business at Santa Fe that needs attention. At least I hope so. I haven't had word from there for weeks."

"Morg, you ought to drop by and route Doc Lewis out of bed and have him look at that bullet burn on Miss Shannon," Alex said. "Everybody was so busy with fainting women they forgot that she was the only one really hurt. There might be infection."

"Fiddle-faddle!" Char said. "It's nothing but a scratch. I don't need a doctor."

Alex drew his pistol from the holster, offered her the

handle of the heavy weapon. "But this is one thing you might need. I imagine you know how to use it."

"Yes," she said calmly. "However, I have one of my own. It belonged to my father. But—but thanks for being so considerate of my welfare. Surely, you don't actually think that shot was meant for me?"

"Maybe," Alex said. "A lot of things are happening that don't seem to make sense."

"Bosh!" Morgan Webb snapped impatiently. "That fellow couldn't have been shooting at you, Char. In the first place, shooting upward through window glass is tricky business. The bullet could have been deflected, and probably was. He may have even been after our friend Len here. Len has manhandled quite a few people in the past. Why in the world would anyone try to kill you?"

"That," Char said, "is what I hope to find out so that I can go gunning for him. I'm the kind that likes to shoot back. I can't believe those bullets were meant for Len. He was well to our right when they were fired."

"It likely was some drunken hoodlum who resented our festive scene and decided to scare us," Webb said.

He seized on his own theory with growing enthusiasm. "Ten to one that's the answer. The old story of the idle poor resenting the idle rich. He probably wasn't aiming at anyone."

Amelia called from where she was waiting in Alex's carriage, "I'm very tired, Alex."

He excused himself, walked to the buggy, and headed the sorrels toward the Thayer home. "I'm sorry I kept you waiting," he said.

"I'm accustomed to being neglected," Amelia said, her attitude sweetly patient, but hurt. She added presently, "Ellis is so much older than I. There is often so little in common for us to talk about."

Alex drove in silence. Amelia spoke again. "You seem to be interested in Charlotte Shannon. That's a rather surprising event in view of the dislike your father had for the Shannons. And doubly so when you remember that Char believes you are responsible for Barney Shannon's death."

"She doesn't believe that," Alex said. "She told me she didn't."

"She told you? How generous of her. I wonder what motive she had——"

"I'm leaving for Santa Fe with the big string the day after tomorrow—or is it tomorrow?" Alex interrupted. "I've lost track of time tonight. It must be past midnight."

"Char is very intelligent, and also discreet," Amelia went on. "Discreet in her sins."

"Let's talk of something else," Alex said.

"We'll talk of Char Shannon and her sins," Amelia said angrily. "She's a cute one, but she's never fooled me. I know and so do other people that Len Capehart——"

"I'm not interested in the private lives of either her or Capehart," Alex said.

"——know that Capehart practically lives at her house, even at night," Amelia rushed on.

Something rebelled within Alex. "I'm sure you're wrong, Amelia."

She laughed. "Let's not bicker about it. Char Shannon isn't that important in our lives." She leaned closer, peering at him in the starlight. That brought her pressing against him. "Or is she?" she demanded challengingly.

"She's important at least as long as she and I are caught in the same grinder," he said. "And also until I've convinced everyone concerned that I didn't have anything to do with that try to burn down their wagon yards that night. Char seems ready to take my word for it. But not Capehart."

He halted the carriage at the gate of Amelia's home, tethered the horses, and helped her down. He walked with her to the door.

In the shadow of the small veranda she suddenly slid her arms around his neck, drew her firm, strong body tight against him, and kissed him.

Then she pushed him away. "Heaven forgive me," she whispered. "If it is sinful even to think of some things, then I am as immoral as I accuse Char Shannon of being in fact."

She opened the door, entered the house, and said softly, "Good night, Alex."

Alex stood a moment, her kiss still warm on his lips, too surprised to move. Then the door was shut.

But before it closed he glimpsed Ellis Thayer sprawled on the parlor sofa, asleep, an empty bottle lying on the carpet beside him. He was unshaven, soggy, unlovely to look at.

He was horrified by this crumbling of Ellis's character. Amelia had implied that her husband had turned to drink as a means of deadening his mind to the conscience which was nagging him because of the way he had sold out the partnership without Alex's knowledge.

Ellis's action, of course, had been unethical, but Alex could hardly believe the man was that sensitive in matters of business. After all, Ellis had never contributed anything to the company except the original five thousand dollars he had invested. He knew little about freighting and had never attempted to learn. Alex doubted that Ellis would be bothered by thoughts of loyalty to the partnership.

He felt that it was something else that had driven Ellis to the bottle. Something big and terrifying.

And Amelia had changed. Or had she? It came to him that the prim, modest person he had known had not been the real Amelia. He had always sensed that there were yearnings and passions in her that were only thinly shielded. Now the shield was slipping and he had seen her, elemental and desirous and ready to be disloyal.

Drawing a long breath, he turned and walked to the buggy and drove away. He was thinking of the vindictiveness in Amelia's voice when she had accused Char Shannon of living in sin with Capehart.

Amelia, he was positive, was utterly wrong. There was an honesty in Charlotte Shannon, a sturdiness of character. From what he had seen of her independent nature he surmised that, were she to care for a man to the point of having an affair with him, it would not be in secret. All the world would know.

The picture returned to his mind of the moment when the gunshots had nearly taken her life.

Morgan Webb, no doubt, had the answer. Surely it must have been some drink-crazed ruffian who had fired for reasons of his own.

Still—he wondered if that shooting had any connection with him and the treasure that he believed was lying out there somewhere beyond the Jornada.

It occurred to him that he had not found a chance to ask Jared Redfield why his father and Barney Shannon had become such bitter opponents when they once had been close friends.

He turned the carriage over to Dan Foss at his wagon yards, then headed on foot toward Hoxie Carver's home. His weariness had moved into every fiber now. Along with his physical exhaustion was an apathy of spirit. He could not put the change in Amelia out of his mind.

He was passing Morgan Webb's wagon yards when Webb pulled in with the surrey in which he had driven Char Shannon home.

Webb had picked up a companion en route to the barn. As they alighted in the dim lantern glow in the tunnel of the structure, Alex saw that it was the man he had seen sitting in Webb's freighting office earlier in the evening—the man whom Hoxie Carver had said was Keno Dane, the professional gun fighter from Texas.

"Damn it, Keno!" Webb was saying in an angry, querulous tone. "I don't want any gunplay here in town. We don't want Hickok to go on the prod against us."

Then Webb glimpsed Alex passing by on the sidewalk, and his voice faded off. When he spoke again his manner was normal—friendly, booming, jovial. "Howdy, Alex. Big night, wasn't it? I can still feel that bubble water. Jared Redfield knows how to entertain."

It was so fatuous that Alex knew Webb had been trying to cover up his previous remark to Keno Dane.

"Good night, Morg," Alex said, and walked onward.

When he reached the Carver house he found Hoxie dressed and moodily drinking black coffee in the kitchen. With him was his wife, wearing a dressing gown, hovering anxiously over him.

"I been in bed once," Hoxie explained. "But had to git up an' go uptown. Fred Moss was killed in a gun fight tonight."

Alex tiredly took the coffee mug. Fred Moss had been a veteran freighter who had worked for Briscoe & Company, for nearly a score of years. Only Hoxie himself had been with the company longer.

"How did it happen?" he asked.

"Keno Dane," Hoxie said bitterly. "Dane was uptown drinkin' and huntin' trouble with freighters from other outfits. He crowded anybody he ran into who worked for us or for Shannon Southwestern. Everybody backed down, not wantin' trouble with a man like him. Everybody, except little Fred. He never was a man to eat crow."

"That's how it was then?" Alex said slowly.

"That's how it was. Fred made the mistake of tryin' to draw first. He wasn't much of a hand with a side gun. He never knew what killed him. Dane blasted him down. Hickok didn't even have an excuse for arrestin' Dane. Everybody who saw it had to admit that Fred went for his gun first."

"Two killings in one night," Alex said wryly. "And self-defense in both cases. I got my man too, you know."

"But there was a considerable difference," Hoxie grunted. "Fred's death was plain murder."

Hoxie added moodily, "That's the start of it. I figured it would turn out this way. Morg Webb brings in killers, an' they're earnin' their pay. It won't be long until you'll have a hard time hirin' a man worth his salt. They'll all have to work for Webb or stand for bein' shoved around by Dane and his crew. Or else go somewhere else."

Alex remembered what Morgan Webb had been saying to Keno Dane when they had alighted from the surrey.

He said slowly, "You called the turn, Hoxie, when you said Morgan was swelling up into a pretty big toad."

9 ⋆ TWO INQUESTS were held the next morning. The first was into the death of Bart Grassman. Alex and Char Shannon were the principal witnesses. Char repeated her statement that Grassman had been the first to go for his gun. Alex was questioned only briefly regarding the cause of the shooting.

Alex said again he was sure Grassman had mistaken him for someone else. That was true enough, for he believed the someone else he referred to had been Len Capehart, and that because he and Capehart were about the same build Grassman had not become aware of his mistake until the last moment there at the gate of the Shannon home.

The jury's verdict was self-defense.

The same panel next held an inquiry into the death of Fred Moss. Alex attended this inquest along with Hoxie Carver. Presently Len Capehart strolled in. They were the only spectators in the shabby little room where the inquest was held.

The way the matter was shunned was a grim tribute to the fear and respect the name of Keno Dane aroused. Few cared to chance offending the man.

Dane himself swaggered in alone after keeping the jury waiting nearly a quarter of an hour. Alex saw that three or four hard-faced men wearing pistols were lingering in the street in the vicinity. Dane's cronies.

Dane packed two six-shooters, but Wild Bill Hickok, who was acting as bailiff, said mildly:

"I'll take the pistols until after the hearing, Keno."

Dane grinned and handed over his revolvers. "That's one way of tamin' me," he said.

Dane was a big, compactly built man, sparsely fleshed, but
56

long-armed, with powerful shoulders. He had large square teeth that were very white against the sun-parched darkness of his skin. His eyes were lusterless black and set deep in the bony structure of his face. Flat, high cheekbones hollowed his face.

The jurors feared him. And the coroner. The inquest was far more perfunctory than Alex's had been. Only two reluctant witnesses were questioned. The verdict was quickly and apologetically rendered. "Self-defense on the part of Keno Dane."

Dane yawned widely and grinned again. "What else could you say?" He shrugged.

He walked to the door, where his guns hung on a peg, and buckled them on. He looked at Alex and Len Capehart. "You're Alex Briscoe, ain't you?" he said. "I hear that you chopped a man down right fast last night yourself. An' there's Len Capehart. How're you, Len? Ain't seen you in years. Abilene, wasn't it? Glad you came to my party. Here's hopin' all of you are alive an' healthy enough to attend my next one."

"There'll be no next one—in Hays City," Wild Bill said. "One's the limit here, Keno."

Dane laughed. "Your luck will run out too someday, Hickok, when the right man comes along."

Dane strolled out then. Alex and Capehart and Hickok also emerged into the street. Char Shannon was sitting in a red-topped, red-wheeled turnout with a team of smart trotters at the tie rail.

She spoke to Alex. "Things got pretty dull the rest of the night last evening. Nobody even tried to take another pot shot at me."

"It might be a good idea to stay away from windows for a while," Alex said.

She shivered a little. "All this is too serious. There's only one thing that will get my mind off it. I'm going down to the Boston Store and buy a new dress. And also a few more practical items for the trip across the Jornada, such as liniment for gnat and mosquito bites and some good stout riding shirts that won't show the dust, and so on. Ugh!"

She set the trotters in stride. She wore a big straw sailor hat. A puff of the hot plains wind snatched it from her head. She caught it on the fly and tossed it on the seat beside her as the trotters whisked her away at a smart clip. Her hair ffew in the breeze.

One of Keno Dane's crew, big, thick-necked, stared, then looked around with a crooked grin and said, "A bold birdie makin' a show o' her shape."

Capehart whirled, drove one punch, and the man hit the dust in the street flat on his back.

Keno Dane, who had been heading for the Gem saloon at the corner, paused and swung around. For a long, breathless moment there was utter silence in the street while Dane calculated the situation.

Dane's dark eyes moved from Capehart to Alex, and then roved on to Hickok. Whatever he saw in their faces convinced him that the sign was not right for resenting what had happened to his man.

He forced a grin and said, "You pack a wallop, Len."

He added, "Someday you'll need it."

Then he walked on and turned through the swing doors into the Gem. Two of his crew picked up the dazed man and carried him into the saloon also.

"That'll be five dollars and costs, Len," Bill Hickok said in his mild manner. "You can post the money at Billy Cravath's justice court. There's an ordinance against disturbing the peace."

Hickok grinned and added, "I'll match you to see which of us pays. Winner buys the drinks."

That afternoon, Alex attended the funeral rites that were held for Fred Moss. And also the brief services at Bart Grassman's grave. The only other attendants at the Grassman burial were Hickok and Len Capehart.

"Well, he lived a hard life," Hickok said as they rode back to town together. "He was the kind that never die in bed."

Afterwards Alex talked with bankers, explaining that he needed leeway. There were no objections. Alex guessed that Jared Redfield had something to do with that willingness.

10 ★ MORGAN WEBB was packing his small leather trunk which he used on wagon trips, selecting shirts and socks and such other items as a man would need on the trail.

His living quarters were in the same long, flat-roofed, frame building at his wagon yards which contained his business office. The building was rambling, and its outer aspect was unpainted and rather shabby. The freighting office was bare and very practical, with a counter and an iron safe and desks, and high stools for the bookkeepers, and brass cuspidors.

His rooms at the rear were expensively, but garishly, furnished. Deep carpets softened the floor of the largest room, and there were oil paintings on the walls—all nudes. The four-poster bed had a velvet canopy and a satin coverlet. A carved sideboard was stocked with liquor and wines. The place was cluttered with heavy chairs and sofas.

A smaller room was equipped partly as a private business office, and one section was partitioned as a small kitchen. Webb employed a Chinese girl as a servant but had sent her away for the day.

Darkness had come. He had eaten a thick steak, along with a bottle of champagne at Shag Hennessy's gambling house. He had tossed a twenty-dollar gold piece on his lucky number, 21, as he had passed the roulette table on his way out. His play had hit. His luck was running.

In the morning he was pulling out with the big wagon string for Santa Fe. He detested the inconveniences of life on the trail, and always had, even though he had been as diligent as any man in his pushing days when he was getting his start.

He was now beginning to build up on his own momentum as a big snowball feeds on its own weight. He could hire men to endure the drudgery and follow the wagons while he enjoyed the comforts of town. In addition he was able to vacation frequently in St. Louis or New Orleans, or occasionally New York, where a man, he felt, could be really civilized.

In fact, he had been planning on another visit to New Orleans, where a dark-eyed Creole girl was waiting. But that would have to be put off now. The snowball was rolling. At a single stroke he had placed Alex Briscoe's freighting company in a position where one little push would send it to ruin and carry Char Shannon and her company with it. Then he could pick up what pieces he wanted for a fraction of their value.

He had worked toward this end ever since he had started in the wagon-freighting business. Even the war had been only an interruption. He professed to have served with the Union Army, but he suspected that some men in Hays knew that he actually had been a guerrilla. In that role he had helped prey on other freighting companies, particularly Briscoe & Company, and had nearly brought it to ruin, while his own wagons, which were being managed by a relative, went unmolested.

Now he was within sight of his objective. Even the unexpected seemed to turn out in his favor. If he could locate the gold and silver that Bart Grassman had lost on the plains, then it would all be his. He would not have to share the major part of the treasure with anyone, now that Grassman and the others were all dead. And he expected Alex Briscoe to lead him to the treasure.

The only flaw had been the killing of Fred Moss by Keno Dane. Webb did not want to antagonize Wild Bill Hickok by flaunting his imported gunmen in the marshal's face here in Hickok's town. There would be plenty of opportunity for browbeating small freighters and wagon men on the trail without risking bringing Hickok and his deadly guns into play against them.

Len Capehart's pistols were enough of a hazard. "And Alex Briscoe might be as fast as Capehart," he had warned Dane the previous night. "From what Char Shannon said, Briscoe was mighty quick on the draw when he burned down Bart Grassman."

"I'll try 'em both on at the right time," Dane had said with his confident grin.

In any event, no real damage had been done by the killing of Fred Moss. Dane had been exonerated, even though he had been placed under a warning by Hickok. In fact, the shooting probably would serve as notice to other men not to oppose Overland Transport and its fighting men.

Webb appraised himself in the mirror. His clothes had been made by the most exclusive tailor in St. Louis. He felt that his shave and haircut left much to be desired, but it was the best Hays City afforded. He decided he was putting on weight. He guessed that he should go a little easy on rich food in the future.

A hand tapped the door. He frowned. It irked him to have to answer doors like a servant. He walked testily to the portal and flung it open.

Then he stared. His visitor was Amelia Thayer.

"Oh, it's you, my dear," he said. "Come in."

Amelia wore a dark coat, and had a veil over her face. She removed these.

She turned up her lips for him to kiss, and he complied in a perfunctory manner. A little malicious flame of resentment began to flicker in her brown eyes.

She looked at the trunk. "Going away, Morgan darling?"

she asked with sugary interest. "To St. Louis, perhaps? Or is it that half-caste wench in New Orleans this time?"

Webb eyed her with searching suspicion. "Your tongue, Amelia," he said, "is as sharp as your mind. However, the fact is that I am going to Santa Fe with the wagon string. On business."

Amelia settled herself in one of the ornate chairs. "Is this business in Santa Fe?" she asked blandly. "Or is it somewhere along the way? Just exactly where, you may not even know. You see, Alex told me last night about Bart Grassman. Alex trusts me."

Webb's smile remained, but it had changed. It was not a smile—merely a fixed expression. "I don't know what you mean, Amelia," he said.

Amelia was smiling too, and her expression was also a mask, covering a determination as unswerving as his own.

"I'm sure you are beginning to know exactly what I mean, Morgan dear," she murmured.

She glanced around and looked at him questioningly. He nodded. "You can talk," he said. "I'm alone."

"Good," Amelia smiled. "There should be no secrets between us. We already know a great deal about each other. Far more than we knew, let us say only little more than twenty-four hours ago."

"And what is it that we've learned?" he asked, picking the words carefully as though sorting them from a box.

"For one thing, you are aware that I no longer respect or love the man I married five years ago," she said.

Webb laughed bitingly. "I've known that some time," he said. "Is that your big secret?"

Amelia answered lightly. "We share another secret. Alex Briscoe, for want of anyone else to suspect, thinks Len Capehart planned the ambush of his treasure wagon. But you and I know that he is wrong, don't we, my dear?"

Webb stood utterly motionless for seconds. "Do we?" he finally said softly.

"Alex isn't aware that you made a flying trip to Santa Fe by stagecoach over the Raton Pass route in the spring. That was after the spring caravan had arrived there, and mail coaches were still getting through. You evidently got wind of that bullion shipment and intended to try to get the contract for Overland Transport. But it had been given to Alex Briscoe. So another plan occurred to you that would make the ride many, many times more profitable."

"You do too much guessing, Amelia."

"I'm sure I'm guessing correctly," she said, unmoved. "You did not allow your presence in Santa Fe to become generally known. And you returned to Hays City on horseback alone in time to have an alibi. You are not the sort of man, Morgan, to risk your fair hair on such a journey unless big money was in sight."

"You also do too much talking, my dear," Webb said.

"You immediately became as thick as thieves with my husband," she went on calmly. "I use the term accurately, I am sure. I am still guessing, of course, but if I am wrong please correct me. You told Ellis you had information that Alex Briscoe would lose his bullion shipment, and that Briscoe & Company would be ruined. You urged Ellis to unload his holdings before the news got out. You knew Char Shannon would buy."

She paused, watching Webb's face, but finding no key to his thoughts there. She moved farther away from him.

"Ellis is a very shallow person," she said. "With weak moral fiber. He never could carry his liquor, but you saw to it that he was supplied while you maneuvered him into helping destroy both Char Shannon and Alex Briscoe. He probably suspected that you had arranged a robbery. The realization came later, after he had sold to Char Shannon, that something else was involved. Murder!"

Their eyes met. Suddenly Webb realized he was confronted by a person whose gaze was as unyielding as his own.

He said, his voice harsh, "Go on."

"It seems that my husband isn't strong enough to stand up under such knowledge," she said. "He is living on alcohol, and is beginning to let his conscience—or rather his fears —get the better of him. He will talk, sooner or later. He is afraid he will be accused of helping in this matter, and will try to save himself. He must be taken out of Hays City at once."

Again their eyes met. "My husband and I are leaving for Santa Fe with the big caravan tomorrow," Amelia went on. "I arranged for the purchase of a wagon and team today so that we can be comfortable. I have let it be known that the trip is for his health, and also that he wants to look over opportunities in Santa Fe to invest the money he realized from the sale of the partnership."

"Does Ellis know about this?"

She shrugged. "Not yet. He is dead-drunk again. When he talks at all he starts mumbling about three dead men. For he was listening the other night when Alex came to our house and told me what had happened to his crew. It'll be easier for all concerned when Ellis is on the trail, where he can't get liquor. He won't be as likely to talk if he is sober."

"You, of course, are willing to face the hardships of the trip for your husband's sake," Webb said ironically.

"Alex Briscoe is the only person alive who knows where his wagons were ambushed," she said. "He will be able to pick up the trail of the bullion without delay."

She paused a moment, then went on:

"From what I've heard of that country along the Cimarron, another person might search a lifetime. Alex trusts me. I'm sure he will confide his plans in me—with a little persuasion. It will be easier to follow him if it is known in advance when he intends to slip away from the wagon train and start his search."

"And what will be your reward?" Webb asked.

"I've never owned a diamond necklace," Amelia said, and a pulse throbbed in her throat and her voice had deepened longingly. "Nor sables, nor servants. I intend to have those things."

She smiled at Webb. "You're to give them to me, Morgan dear. Now, isn't that scandalous? Me, a married woman, deciding such a thing?"

Webb was staring at her with the same terrible fascination she had seen so often lately in her husband's eyes. This pleased her, and she laughed softly. "You seem startled, darling," she said. "And angry. Don't attempt anything rash —such as a repetition of the Jared Redfield incident, for instance."

"What are you talking about?" Webb demanded thickly.

"Fortunately for you," she murmured, "I was the only person who noticed that you were missing from the car at the time those shots were fired. You had drifted away a few moments earlier and had slipped outside by way of the rear platform."

Webb tried to speak—and failed. Amelia laughed again gleefully. "You are a fool, Morgan," she said. "Killing Jared Redfield would probably have been a fatal blunder for you. You might have been suspected. Everyone knew you were disgruntled because Redfield had delayed awarding the grading job. Yes, I overheard. I sat near the curtain when the confab was going on, and eavesdropped."

Contempt now came into her face as she watched him. "Fortunately for you, your hand must have trembled then, just as it does now," she went on. "Your bullet came within

63

a shade of killing Char Shannon. Everyone knows you're smitten on her, and would like nothing better than to marry her. It diverted suspicion from you. It never occurred to anyone that Redfield had been the real target. You must control those angry impulses, Morgan. It convinced me that you need someone to advise you."

"And you're that person?" Webb jeered.

She walked to his liquor cabinet and poured herself a tiny glass of sherry. She sipped it a moment.

"If you are considering shooting at other persons," she said, "me, for instance, I must tell you, darling, that I have set down in my own handwriting everything I know and suspect about that treasure shipment. It is in a sealed envelope and is stored in our strongbox in a vault at the bank. It will be opened only in case of my death by violence."

She beamed at Webb. Her brittle coldness faded now, and she smoothed her hair and adjusted her bonnet and gazed into the mirror before donning the concealing veil. She was again a decorous, composed young matron. For she was sure of her mastery over him.

"With the two of us working together," she said, "Overland Transport will become something to be reckoned with. Mr. Redfield told me Char Shannon plans to shift their business into railroad holdings. I think it an excellent idea, and we should follow it."

"You bitch!" Webb snarled, almost admiringly.

Lifting the veil, she kissed him. "Good night, dear," she said. "I hardly imagine you will dream about that girl in New Orleans tonight, or the one in St. Louis either. You have someone else to think about. Me!"

Then she left him.

11 ★ WALNUT CREEK and the Pawnee Fork, milestones of the trail, were astern, and the sand flats marking the broad Arkansas River quivered ahead in the heat waves. The buffalo grass lay brown and dry beneath the August sun. Dust spooned up by the heavy wheels of fifty laden prairie wagons and hundreds of hooves formed a great yellow banner to windward of the column.

It was still fairly safe to travel in double file, and thereby at least half of the drivers could stay clear of the dust, and had only the blazing sun as their tribulation. Later on they would be three and four abreast and in compact formation, with the line of flankers doubled. For soon there must be opponents far more merciless than the weather with which to contend.

For this was only the fourth day on the trail, and the caravan was now just beginning to shake down into the raw and grinding mile-by-mile routine.

The travelers were starting the mighty sweep southwestward up the great bend of the Arkansas. Here they were within reach of Fort Larned, but from here on each mile would carry them deeper into the Indian country, with only Fort Dodge as an isolated island of safety in the vastness of the plains ahead. West of Dodge they would cross the Arkansas into the Jornada.

Alex rode as a flanker. Mounted on a rangy roan, he, along with other men, paralleled the course of the wagons at a quarter of a mile distance on either side. They rode mainly on the crests of the swells, but they also investigated coulees and bluffs or other items of natural cover that might conceal a foe.

It was monotonous traveling, for they were forced to hold to the lumbering pace of the wagons, but it also had its spice, for it was a task at which a man might lose his scalp.

While it was unlikely they would encounter Indians in strength this close to the military post, Zack Dixon, the plainsman who had been hired to scout for the wagon train, had found signs that small hunting parties were in the vicinity. The Indians were keeping tab on the caravan.

However, old gray-bearded Joe Wallace, who had been elected captain of the wagon train at the organization meeting the first night out of Hays, still permitted the loose double formation.

The vehicles were strung out for more than half a mile. The great, curving canvas tilts, miraged high above the swells in the shimmering heat waves, were for all the world like billowing sails. The prairie itself seemed to undulate beneath the sun. The tracks of wagons which had traveled this route in the past formed the only guiding mark across the face of this grassy ocean—the only assurance that other men had ever passed this way.

Alex had seen this sight many times. It always stirred him. The trail was his heritage. He had first gone down to

65

Santa Fe with his father when he was four years old. He had traveled the bleak Jornada, and had covered the longer route by way of Bent's Fort and Raton Pass many times.

He had never known his mother, for she had died the day he was born. He had only a picture of her, framed in heavy Mexican silver, which his father had given him. The picture was that of a winsome, dark-haired, beautiful young woman of nineteen in her wedding gown.

And now his father was gone also, sleeping these three years in a lonely grave on the brown plains near Wagon Mound, far beyond the Jornada, on the trail to Santa Fe. Alex and Tom Briscoe had been side by side, helping stand off a thrust on their wagons by raiding Apaches when an arrow had struck his father in the chest.

Alex had wielded one of the spades that had filled the grave, and he had felt that it had been a holy thing to do, for he and his parent had been comrades as well as father and son.

He thought of the bitter grudge that had endured between his father and Barney Shannon. He believed Hoxie Carver could tell him the cause of that feud. But Hoxie was back at Hays, helping unite the interest of Briscoe & Company and of Shannon Southwestern.

Alex had proposed that arrangement. "We may as well combine operations at once, for the sake of economy at least," he had said. And Char had agreed.

Under that same arrangement, she and Alex had five wagons in the caravan, traveling under the new firm name of Briscoe & Shannon. Four of these vehicles carried freight which had been contracted through to Santa Fe by both companies during the summer.

The fifth wagon, as far as the other members of the caravan were concerned, was loaded with cargo for Santa Fe also. But the cases and barrels it contained were empty of anything except provisions for two men, a few sacks of grain, and spare rifles and ammunition. The wagon, slightly smaller than average, was drawn by a picked team of six matched duns.

True to her word, Char Shannon was with the caravan. Alex still resented the presence of the dark-haired girl, for he felt she was there to keep an eye on him. There was stiff constraint between them.

Morgan Webb also had five wagons in line, loaded with consignments for Santa Fe, and with trade goods for El Paso and Chihuahua. Webb, flashily garbed, and wearing a cream-colored hat, was accompanying his wagons in person, and had brought along four thoroughbred saddle horses.

In addition to his regular wagon crews Keno Dane and six of the tough gunmen whom Webb had imported into Hays City were along as a special escort for his wagons.

The addition of this group of hard-bitten fighting men to the strength of the company had been hailed as further insurance against Indian attack. At the start of the journey Webb had been regarded as a benefactor. Now the wagon people were not so sure. They were wondering if Keno Dane and his truculent, swaggering crew might not be more dangerous than the Indians.

And then there was Amelia Thayer. Alex had been astounded when he discovered that she and her husband were traveling to Santa Fe also.

She had gazed at him shyly when he had first come riding to her wagon. There had been warming color in her throat, and he believed she was remembering the intimacy of that moment when she had kissed him so purposely.

She explained why she and her husband were making the trip. Certainly Ellis needed some sort of a change of scene. From the glimpses Alex had of him as he lay in their wagon he had deteriorated shockingly. He displayed all the symptoms of a person attempting to taper off of a debauch—and failing.

Amelia permitted him to be up and about for only short periods, and never let him move more than a few steps from their wagon. She was always at his side, warding off persons who attempted to stop and chat.

She particularly refused to let Alex come near her husband. "Stay away from him just a few days more, Alex dear," she insisted. "The sight of you seems to excite him terribly. He has delusions of guilt about selling the partnership. He's been drinking so hard he has hallucinations. Sometimes he even raves about being responsible for the deaths of your men in that shooting on the trail."

"You told him?" Alex asked frowning.

"Yes," she sighed. "It was a mistake. I know that now. But he would have found it out eventually. He gets things mixed. Sometimes he mumbles that you were responsible for the ambush. Then——"

"Me? Why does he think that?"

"It's all in his mind, of course, Alex. Then in the next breath he'll be accusing people like Wild Bill Hickok, or Barney Shannon, who is dead, or even Jared Redfield or Morgan Webb, of all people. He uses any name that comes to mind. I'm telling you all this so that you'll be prepared for anything he says."

"I understand," Alex had said.

"I'm praying that this journey will bring him back to sanity," Amelia had said, and tears had suddenly began streaking down her cheeks. "But I am beginning to fear his mind is permanently affected. I am trying to lead him away from drinking, but that is much more difficult than I had anticipated."

Amelia had spent money making her wagon comfortable. It was fitted with an easy chair and a dressing table with a mirror, and two comfortable pallets and a rug. Portable steps could be dropped into place for easy access.

She had hired a driver and a swamper. They were hard-mouthed individuals, who packed holster guns. Zack Dixon, the scout, whom Alex had known since boyhood, had confirmed the general opinion of them.

"They're tied in with Keno Dane an' his bunch of leppies," Zack had told Alex. "I reckon Mrs. Thayer didn't sabe what kind o' striped cats they was when she hired 'em."

Amelia always remained in the wagon, close to her husband's side on the trail. She would sit in the easy chair, fanning herself. She had told Alex, with a brave smile, that she was happy to endure any discomfort for Ellis's sake. She said that her only fear was that her strength would not hold out all the way to Santa Fe.

"These plains will beat you down, smother you, if you let them," Alex had warned her. "You'll get so that you will want to hide in this wagon all the time. You've got to come to grips with this country. Get out and walk with the wagons. Crush the grass under your feet and feel your own strength. Sweat and swear and taste dust."

Amelia had looked ill. "How vulgar you've become, Alex," she had said. "The trail brutalizes a person if you permit it to do so. I assure you I shall not let it matter to me."

Alex wished Amelia had more of the capacity for accepting situations that was displayed by Char Shannon. Char Shannon, of course, had been over the trail many times, and knew its discomforts and its hazards.

She had a sunburned nose and was beginning to sprout a crop of freckles that horrified her, but she had never uttered a word of complaint in spite of the heat and dust.

Right at this moment, to the delight of the crews, she was vying with some of the drivers in the art of swinging a bullwhip, a form of recreation that often occupied the wagon men even though there were no ox-drawn vehicles with the company. Only horses and mules were being used for the sake of speed.

She wore a light calico blouse, and held the hem of her riding skirt clear of her boots by the wrist loop while she swung the whip lustily. An incongruous costume, but on her figure any garment had grace and shape.

Again, from Alex's own youth came the memory of watching covertly from a distance while Char, a slip of a girl, had also practiced with a heavy bullwhip in the shade of her father's wagons in the dusty old plaza at Santa Fe.

It was all as clear in his mind as yesterday, and with it came the nostalgic yearning for time to turn back. He saw again the great prairie wagons towering above the slender girl in calico. There was the long, flat-roofed palace with its cool, shadowed gallery, and the cathedral looking down. And he heard again the tap of a dancer's heels in one of the cantinas and the pulse of the stringed music—and the crack of that bullwhip that seemed almost too big for her to lift. He remembered his own wistful loneliness, for he had been eighteen then, and Santa Fe had been a long way from Independence.

Char suddenly turned and gazed at him. Even at that distance Alex became aware of a singleness of thought and knew she also had been remembering that hot and dreamy July day in Santa Fe. Her eyes had been drawn to him by that recollection.

She mounted her mouse-colored mare and came loping impulsively toward him. Joe Wallace, who was riding ahead of the wagons, rose in the stirrups and turned to wave her back. The captain's word was law, and it was forbidden for any of the company except the flankers to leave the line of march without permission. Then Joe thought better of it, and pretended he had not noticed this infraction.

Alex saw the softness of these recollections in her dark eyes as she joined him. A wide-brimmed Mexican straw sombrero shaded her face, held by a braided chin strap. A Henry rifle was thrust in a scabbard from the side saddle. It had a carved stock, inlaid with brass.

Alex spoke abruptly. "You knew I was watching you that day at the plaza."

"So you really were thinking of the same thing as I just now," she said, a run of delight in her voice. "There really must be such a thing as this mind reading that they talk about. Yes, I knew. As a matter of fact, I'm afraid I was showing off for your benefit. But I pretended I was unaware you existed. That was not the only time I went out of my way to ignore you."

Alex laughed. The constraint faded—for the moment at least. For once he felt at east in her presence. He reached for his tobacco pouch and brown papers and rolled a smoke. "Do you mind?" he asked.

They had moved beyond a knoll which hid them from the wagons. She took the pouch and papers from his hand and her quick fingers fashioned a cigarette with a dexterity that showed considerable practice.

She saw the disapproval in his face as she lit the quirlie with one of his matches. She chuckled without penitence. "I only wish I had the courage to come right out in public with my hidden vices," she said. "Len Capehart has me cowed. He looked like he wanted to take a quirt to me that night I shocked the ladies at the Redfield party by smoking. But they were all acting so stuffy. I wanted to give them a jolt."

"You place high value on Capehart's opinion," Alex said. "Are you in love with him?"

She stiffened. She tilted back her head, looking at him narrowly down over her nose.

"I see the purpose in that question," she said reflectively. "Your point is that a woman in love can't judge a man clearly. You're warning me that you still believe Len was back of the robbery of your wagons."

Alex said nothing. They were now rounding into view of the caravan again. Char snuffed out her cigarette.

A commotion was taking place toward the middle of the column where the five wagons belonging to Alex and Char were.

Alex arose in the stirrups. It was a fist fight. One of the combatants went down. The victor was Keno Dane, the gun fighter.

Dane drove the toe of a boot viciously into the ribs of his dazed opponent. Then the man walked with his bravo stride to his horse, mounted, and rode casually down the line of wagons.

Char Shannon said angrily, "That looks like Tim Murphy that Keno Dane beat up this time. Yesterday it was Pete Sugarman. And ours isn't the only outfit he is picking on. He and that crowd of ruffians Morgan Webb has hired are drunk half the time and hunting trouble with our men."

70

Alex saw Dane look in his direction as though inviting a challenge.

The caravan, which had ground to a halt during the fight, lurched ahead again. Alex signaled to the other flankers that he was leaving his position, and rode to the wagon in which Tim Murphy had been placed. This vehicle had pulled out of line and was not in motion. Two men were working on the injured mule skinner.

"Broken jaw, an' it looks like he's got some busted ribs too," a swamper said sourly. "Dane put the boots to him. He outweighs Tim by thirty pounds, an' is twenty years younger. Tim's pushin' sixty."

"What started it?"

"Dane deliberately forced it on Tim, jest like he's started trouble with other men. He crowds you until you eat dirt or fight. Then you find that you're overmatched whether it's with fists or shootin' ar'ns. All them other roughs that work for Webb follow the same tactics. It's gittin' so a man has to talk mighty small to stay healthy around that outfit."

Alex looked around. Len Capehart had arrived and was standing, a thumb hooked in his gun belt, his weathered, dusty hat pulled low over his eyes. The only others present were Char and three or four men from their wagons. Even Joe Wallace was avoiding this issue and staying carefully in his place as pilot.

As captain, it should have been Wallace's responsibility to investigate the row and to mete out discipline to the instigator, for the caravan, because of the Indian danger, was operating under a written pact which each member had signed, binding him to rules of conduct that were almost as rigid as a military code. Dane and his followers were deriding Wallace's authority.

Alex remembered what Hoxie Carver had told him back at Hays. "The first thing a man who wants to be top dog does is to try to put the fear of wrath in everybody else," Hoxie had said. "Once he gits everybody crawlin' around afraid of him, then he grabs everything that's loose for himself an' runs things his own way."

Alex now looked at Capehart. "Dane's hand has got to be called," he said.

"Tough man." Capehart shrugged. "He knows all the tricks."

"Nevertheless, it has to be done. Will you keep the rest of his pack off me?"

71

Capehart drew a gold piece from his pocket. "Heads you take him on," he said, "tails I try my luck."

Alex caught the coin in the air and handed it back to Capehart without looking at it. "Tim Murphy worked for me, remember," he said. "So did poor Fred Moss back at Hays."

Capehart slowly pocketed the coin, and Alex endured his scrutiny. Whatever Capehart saw in his face seemed satisfactory, for he nodded. "I'll keep 'em off you. When do you aim to brace him?"

"The next time he tries to crowd somebody," Alex said. "Then there won't be any doubt as to my purpose."

Char stood gazing, deeply troubled. She started to say something, then seemed to decide it was useless.

Tim Murphy was made as comfortable as possible, and Alex waved the wagon ahead to its position in line.

The vehicle owned by Amelia and her husband, its flaps down in spite of the afternoon heat, came abreast as Alex mounted and wheeled his horse, intending to return to his place as a flanker.

At that moment the rear flap was violently parted. Ellis, a wild, unshaven, haggard figure, clad only in a nightshirt, was visible, struggling with Amelia in the open rear bow.

"Alex! Alex!" Ellis began screeching. He fought free of Amelia's grasp, leaped from the moving wagon, and fell sprawling. He got to his feet and staggered toward Alex.

"Listen to me!" he croaked, his lungs sobbing with the desperation of his efforts. "Alex, for God's sake watch yourself! They mean to——"

Alex swung his horse, intending to hurry to Ellis's assistance, but at that moment Morgan Webb, riding one of his thoroughbreds, raced in ahead of him. Webb left the saddle, caught Ellis in his arms, and carried him with almost brutal speed and strength back toward Amelia's wagon.

Alex started to dismount, but Amelia motioned him back. "No, Alex," she said. "It's the sight of you that excites him. Let Morgan take care of him."

Ellis twisted around, looked up into the face of the man who was carrying him bodily. He suddenly seemed to go limp. He offered no further resistance, and Amelia and Webb together lifted him into the wagon and carried him to a pallet.

Amelia dropped the flap, shutting out all view of the interior.

Alex slowly mounted and rode away. Char had been sit-

72

ting on her horse, watching this. She was now moving away also, but there was perplexity in her face.

He rode to her side. He kept remembering the look in Ellis's sunken eyes. They had burned with a wild and frenzied glare. There had been no doubt about that. But Alex could not shake off the impression that those had not been the eyes of a man out of his senses.

"I wonder what Mr. Thayer was talking about," Char said, her eyes grave.

"He was out of his head," Alex said, his voice suddenly rough with irritation.

"He seemed to be trying to warn you about something, or against someone," she said.

"Amelia told me yesterday that he was making all kinds of wild statements about everybody," Alex said.

"Who, for instance?"

"Me. Wild Bill Hickok. Redfield. Anyone whose name came to mind."

She swung the horse to ride away, then paused, looking at him over her shoulder. "If—if you have to fight with Keno Dane," she said, choosing her words carefully, "fight him with fists, not—not pistols. He's—he's deadly with a gun, they say."

"I savvy," Alex said. "If I were to cash in my checks, you might have difficulty finding that bullion. I'm of some value to Shannon Southwestern—alive."

She whirled her horse, brought it alongside again. Before Alex could perceive her intention, she slapped him with all the violence she could muster.

The print of her hand was a white, hard brand on his cheek. She was waiting, her face ashen, her eyes dark and defiant.

"All right," she said huskily. "That was a cowardly thing on my part, hitting you when you didn't expect it. However, you may slap me if you wish. It will make me feel better, at least. I'm ashamed of letting go of my temper. I vowed that I'd keep it under control the rest of my life."

She added, "But you had it coming. You know that."

She waited a moment longer, and when she saw that he was not going to speak she spurred away, galloping to overtake the wagons, which were now beginning the classic maneuver that would form the frontier circle at the overnight campsite that had been selected.

The sun was sinking, and the shallow waters of the Arkansas glinted like gold to the south of the trail.

Alex watched Keno Dane ride his horse over bedrolls of Char Shannon's drivers, which had been unloaded from a wagon as camp was set up. When one man objected, Dane squirted tobacco juice on his boots.

It's coming fast, Alex reflected. Tonight, most likely.

12 ★ SOMEONE BEGAN scraping a fiddle as the evening meal was finished and darkness settled. A freighter started a buck and wing, and more fuel was piled on the central fire.

Char dragged red-faced Zack Dixon into the circle and commenced bowing and scraping before him until Zack got over his embarrassment and started showing her a thing or two in the way of cutting a caper.

Others joined in. Feminine partners were scarce, for there were only Char and the wives of three immigrants on hand. Nevertheless, the circle was filled with activity, for it was in all their minds that there would be little chance for gaiety the remainder of the way.

Alex stood in the shadow of a wagon, a foot on a hub, taking no part in the merriment. Char was dancing with a freighter. Then Morgan Webb cut in. It seemed to Alex that she hesitated a moment before accepting him as a partner. Alex found himself approving. Evidently Webb's courtship was not progressing.

Len Capehart was her partner for the next number. The Tennessean moved with the ease of a supple man. Char was all animation. They made a handsome couple. Alex, somehow, no longer found himself enjoying the scene.

In the next moment he had something else to think about. Keno Dane had just joined the circle of onlookers. Alex's body tightened.

Dane wore his brace of six-shooters and was followed by three members of his crew as he strolled along. Occasionally he made some jeering remark. Now and then he pushed men roughly aside who did not move out of his way. He had come here to continue his campaign to domineer the wagon company.

Capehart swung by with Char, and Alex met his glance. Capehart was also watching Keno Dane. So was Char. Her eyes showed worry.

74

Dane's presence was casting a damper on the festivities. The fiddler lost enthusiasm. Tension began to clamp down on the dancers. The gathering thinned.

Alex stood watching and waiting. He carried the right-hand gun of a brace of matched navy pistols that he had bought before leaving Hays. These were cap-and-ball weapons, which he preferred because of their weight and balance over the more cumbersome Dragoon .44's. The Navy's .36 caliber was more than sufficient for stopping a human being.

But Dane had not yet given cause for serious challenge. However, it was coming.

There was the rustle of skirts, and Alex turned. Amelia came out of the darkness. She said in a hurt voice, "I was so lonely. I couldn't stand it a minute longer in that wagon when everyone else was being so happy. You've neglected me terribly, Alex."

"Intentionally on this occasion, at least, Amelia," he said.

"That's an odd apology, I must say," she said.

"This shindig might not end as happily as you think," he said. "However, now that you're here and all gussied up, we'll dance. But I'm afraid we'll have to pay the fiddler before long."

She didn't understand. He led her into the light and swung her into step with the quavering fiddle. He kept Keno Dane in sight.

"You could, at least, pay some attention to me!" Amelia whispered angrily, and he felt her fingernails bite through his shirt. "Whatever are you staring at? After all, I'm not that repulsive. You——"

It came then. Char Shannon was dancing with a trader named Ed Jarvis, who had cut in on Morgan Webb. Now Keno Dane walked into the circle, crowding other dancers aside.

"Cuttin' in!" Dane said loudly, and brought the palm of his hand down on Jarvis' back with staggering force. The blow sent Jarvis to his knees, breathless. He was an amiable man of middle age and of medium height, but he came to his feet, raging, and swung a fist at the gunman.

Dane had anticipated that. He evaded the blow and smashed Jarvis in the face with a brutal punch. Jarvis reeled off balance and Dane moved in, his face wicked as he measured his man for punishment. He meant to slash and maim.

But Alex stepped between them and shoved Dane roughly back.

"Ed's no more of a match for you than Tim Murphy was, Keno," he said. "Or Fred Moss."

Keno Dane moved back another pace, and stood with his long arms loose at his side. He was set on a hair-trigger readiness to go for his guns.

"Do you figure you're more my size, Briscoe?" he asked.

"By any measurement," Alex answered. "Guns, fists, knives. You name it."

There was a rush of feet as bystanders scattered away from them. The three gunmen who had followed Dane suddenly formed a solid unit. From the corner of an eye Alex noted that Char Shannon still stood little more than an arm's length from him. She would not pay Keno Dane the tribute of moving away from his threat of gunfire.

Len Capehart's voice spoke from the background. "This is between Briscoe and Dane. Everybody else stay out of it. I'll chime in against the first one that interferes."

Capehart stood with his back to a wagon, a brace of pistols in his hands.

Morgan Webb came striding up. "No gunplay!" he said loudly, urgently. "If you two men have some grudge against each other, then settle it with your fists. And settle it somewhere else. I, for one, prefer to resume the dance."

Dane carefully lifted his hands until they were well above his guns and clear of them. "Fists suit me," he said. "Come on, Briscoe."

"We'll stay here, Keno," Alex said. "This is as good a place as any, and there's more light. I have a hunch you know your way around in the dark too well. Morg can keep right on dancing if he isn't interested."

He unbuckled his gun belt and hung it over a wagon tongue, and laid aside his hat. Dane removed his guns and hat, and stripped off his shirt.

He outweighed Alex by some twenty pounds by appearances. His shoulders were high-set and bunched with sinew.

"He'll knee and kick and butt," Capehart murmured. "I've seen him fight. Keep him moving. Walk around him. He's packing a little tallow around the middle. He'll slow down."

Then he exclaimed, "Here he comes!"

Dane was charging, thinking Alex was not set. He came across the circle with a rush, weaving, his fists low and ready.

Alex knew this was to be a camp-style fight, with nothing barred, including gouging and maiming.

He faded aside, sliding clear of the punches Dane threw. He caught the man with a left that gashed a cheekbone.

76

Dane whirled and kicked with agility. Even though Alex had anticipated something like this and had shifted around, he could not entirely evade that maneuver. The toe of Dane's boot drove into the taut muscles of his left thigh. He endured agony. The sinews in his leg knotted.

He reeled back, the leg unable to support him. Dane came upon him, punching savagely. Alex felt blood in his mouth, was aware of its warmness on his face.

He dropped suddenly to the ground, pivoting his body and thrusting out with both feet at the same moment, catching Dane at the knees and knocking his legs from under him.

Dane's forward impetus carried him over Alex and the man landed on his back almost in the fire with a crash that sent the breath wheezing from him.

Alex was unable to take advantage of that chance, and Dane regained his feet. Dane was fast and resilient. Nevertheless, he had been shaken and he stalled for time. They circled, and Alex felt the numbness fade from his thigh.

He seized the initiative. He moved in, feinting, jabbing, circling. He baited Dane into lifting his guard—and then weaved in and sank his right fist savagely into the body just above the belt.

Dane tried to clinch, but his clawing hands only found Alex's shirt, ripping it from his shoulders. Alex backed away, then came in again, punching. Dane covered his body this time, but his face paid the penalty. His nose changed to a flattened, bloody mass. Blood spurted from a slashed jaw.

Dane lurched in desperately, and Alex could not evade him this time. Long arms wrapped around him. He felt Dane's fingers creeping to his face, probing for the eyes.

He lifted Dane bodily, plunged forward half a dozen paces, carrying the weight aloft, and smashed his man's back against a wagon hub.

That could have broken the spine of a lesser person. Dane survived that, but now he was retching and gagging and fading. Alex tore free of the man's grasp. His head was swimming, his heart straining. His own blood partly blinded him. There were raw and ugly welts on his body.

They traded punches. Dane clenched again. They fell to the ground. Alex rammed an elbow into Dane's throat, forcing the man's head back until he broke free.

Alex got to his knees and drove two short jabs to the face. Keno Dane fell slowly back, collapsing on the trampled earth, and lay there, breathing with whistling effort through puffed, gory lips.

Alex walked on rubbery legs to a wagon and clutched the spokes of a wheel and hung on, gasping. Presently he looked at Morgan Webb. "You can go on with the dance now, Morg," he said.

Dane's gunmen moved in and carried his sagging form away. One of them looked at Alex and said, "It won't be fists the next time, mister. You'll find that Keno gits tougher the more you try him out."

Alex felt hands supporting him. "Help me, Len," Char Shannon was saying. "We'll take him to our tent."

Alex forced himself to stand on his own feet. "I can make it on my own," he said. "Thanks."

He looked around. Amelia was not present. She had fled to her wagon when the fight started.

In the small tent which served as Char's sleeping quarters she bent close in the lanternlight, using an alum stick and a purifying solution on Alex's injuries. Stitches were needed to close a gash on his jaw. She performed this task with sure fingers, her breath brushing his ear as she worked.

Their eyes met at close range and held. Alex was suddenly asking himself a startling and unanswerable question. He saw something of this same surprise in her gaze. She returned to her task, but with some confusion.

She got out his tobacco and papers, rolled a smoke, lighted it, and placed it between his lips, for his hands were too battered and swollen for that task.

"Thank you," she said.

"For what?" Alex demanded.

"For whipping that repulsive, ugly man-eater. In fact, you practically annihilated him."

Len Capehart abruptly walked out of the tent into the darkness. Alex saw a taut and almost hostile bitterness in his face. Char lapsed into silence.

She finished her task. Alex got to his feet and said, "Thanks! I feel like a man with a new face."

She said soberly, "Dane will try to kill you at first chance. You know that."

Again they stood gazing at each other. Color rose in her face. They both were recalling that it was a similar remark that had led to her slapping him that afternoon.

"I was wrong today," Alex said. "I——"

A gunshot slammed through the camp. Shouts rose. Alex heard the men on picket duty calling to each other in the darkness beyond the wagon circle and counting off their posts to make sure the cordon was still intact.

78

A woman screamed wildly. Amelia's voice. Alex began running.

A group had gathered around an object which lay on the ground not far from Amelia's wagon. Alex pushed through the circle. Someone arrived with a lighted lantern.

Ellis Thayer, wearing a nightshirt, lay there, his body huddled in a pattern of agony. Amelia was crouching on her knees beside him, uttering small, whimpering sounds of terror.

Blood showed on the chest of her husband's garb. But the splotch was not spreading, for Ellis's pulse was stilled.

A rifle began exploding somewhere beyond the wagons. Three shots were fired, the muzzle flames etching out the arched tops of the wagons.

Then silence. Alex helped Amelia to her feet and turned her over to the women who had arrived.

Morgan Webb, carrying a rifle, came hurrying into the light. "I sighted the devil as he ran over a rise beyond camp," he said. "I smoked him up, but don't know whether I got him or not. We'll find out in the morning. A man might get a war ax through his skull if he went scouting around out there in the dark. Or a lance in his belly. There likely aren't many of 'em, and they'll be as hard to catch as eels."

"An Injun killed Ellis?" someone asked hoarsely.

"Of course! Who else would pick off a man from the dark? Ellis was delirious again, and had jumped from the wagon. Amelia was trying to overtake him and calm him down when it happened. Poor fellow. He chose the wrong time to wander from his bed."

Alex walked to Amelia's wagon nearby. Char and two other women of the company were with her. A lantern hung in the bow. Amelia lay on the pallet, a fixed, glassy look in her eyes. It might have been terror. Or shock.

She saw Alex and started to say something. Then she burst into a storm of weeping. She seemed to be looking at something just behind him. He turned. Only Morgan Webb stood there. Webb still held the rifle, and now he removed his hat.

"I'm terribly sorry about your husband, Mrs. Thayer," he said. "Is there anything I can do?"

Amelia began weeping loudly. Char made a warning gesture, and both Webb and Alex went away.

Alex, afterwards, walked beyond the wagons to the picket line. A quarter moon rode the sky, but in its faint light he could make out no ridge or rise on which an escaping Indian might have been sky-lined. The area was flat sagebrush.

A slight sound caused him to turn. His bandaged hand darted to his holster—and only then did he realize how vulnerable he was, for he could not have lifted the gun, so swollen were his fingers.

Against the glow of the wagon fires he identified the man who had come up behind him so silently. Once again it was Morgan Webb.

"Better wear boots instead of moccasins, my friend," Alex said. "Someone might mistake you for an Indian."

"Maybe you're right," Webb agreed. "I forgot I was wearing the damned things. I carry them to rest my feet after a day in saddle boots, and had slipped them on just before the excitement started. Well, I hope that's the end of the trouble. You were a little rough on Keno, Alex. After all, he was half drunk and hardly responsible."

"Tell him then to stay sober," Alex said. "If he crowds anyone in this company again, I'll look him up once more. And I'll be much rougher the next time."

The joviality faded out of Webb. "You're packing a chip on your shoulder, Alex," he said. "I'm afraid it might grow into a coffin for you someday."

"I've misjudged you, Morg," Alex said.

"So?" Webb said silkily. "In what way?"

"Maybe you saw to it that you were misjudged. I never figured you as dangerous. Maybe I took on the wrong man when I mixed with Keno Dane. Maybe next time I'll correct that mistake."

"You can't afford to make any more mistakes," Webb murmured chidingly. "Good night, Alex."

Then he walked away. Alex stood thoughtfully watching the shadow of his erect figure merge with the shapes of the wagons.

He turned and walked through camp toward his own bed, for he was slated to stand the last trick on picket duty.

Len Capehart stepped out of the darkness a dozen paces behind him and maintained that distance as Alex picked his way past wagons and picket stakes and equipment.

Alex knew Capehart was there but said nothing until he reached his destination. He waited beside one of his wagons until the Tennessean came up. He said, "Why?"

Capehart shrugged. "Char told me it might be a good idea. I thought so too. Some of Dane's pals might decide to eliminate you. You're too valuable to lose—right now at least, Briscoe."

"Did Miss Shannon say that?"

"No," Capehart said. "It was my own thought." He rolled and lighted a cigarette, and added casually, "Morg Webb must have eyes like an owl. It's mighty dark out there."

"So I noticed," Alex said.

Char came walking back, returning from Amelia's wagon. Peering, she identified them in the shadows and joined them. "Amelia will be all right," she said. "I gave her something to help her sleep. She seems calm enough."

She hesitated a moment, then said, "Almost too calm. I——" She halted, debating whether to say more, and decided against it.

She said hastily, "Good night, Len. Good night, A—Alex."

She moved away toward the tent. It was the first time she had used Alex's given name.

Suddenly he left Capehart and overtook her. He laid a hand on her arm, halting her. "You don't believe I had anything to do with the fire that night, do you?" he breathed tautly.

She turned toward him, but he could not see her expression in the shadows. "No," she said. "I told you I never believed that, and I don't. The Shannons and the Briscoes were never the kind to strike from the dark. It was you, yourself, who tried to put the accusation on my lips, remember. Someone else must have put the thought in your mind that I believed you were the one."

Alex was silent a moment. "Yes," he finally said. "And thanks."

He was recalling that it was Amelia who had let him understand that Char Shannon believed he was the cause of her father's death. He asked a question that seemed to have no bearing on what had gone before. "What started that grudge between my father and yours?"

"You really don't know?" Char asked, surprised.

"No. But it doesn't seem to be a secret to anyone except me. Jared Redfield and Hoxie Carver know. And you also, apparently."

She hesitated. "It was a woman," she finally said. "What else could part strong men who had been such friends?"

"Who was she?"

"They were both in love with her. But she married Tom Briscoe."

Alex said numbly, "My mother?"

"Your mother." Char Shannon nodded. "It was not her fault. She loved your father. She did not love Barney Shannon. But Barney Shannon was a headstrong, proud man. My father never forgave her or your father. And his bitterness only deepened when your mother died the day you were born. He blamed you for that, and he blamed your father."

She stood broodingly quiet for a moment. Then she said, "Dad married my lovely mother two years later and worshiped her. But he never forgave Tom Briscoe, nor you, for your mother's death. My mother tried many times to bring them together again. She failed. She told me about it before she died when I was a child. It was such a pity."

She said again, "What else could part strong friends, but a woman?"

Her eyes were shining with tears. "Now you've got me crying over it again," she choked. "Too many tears have been shed already because of the stubbornness of two proud men. First it was your own mother, and then mine, who wept. And now they are gone—all four of them, and there is no use regretting the lost years of bitterness. And still I weep over it and can't stop the tears when I start thinking about them. Never bring this matter up again, Alex Briscoe."

She turned and fled sobbing to the tent.

Len Capehart spoke at Alex's side, his voice a hard thread, devoid of all emotion. "You have all the luck, Briscoe."

13 ★ NO TRACE of Indians could be found near the camp at daybreak. If it really had been an Indian at whom Morgan Webb had fired his shots had not found their target.

They dug a grave in the sagebrush and buried Ellis Thayer in the hot plains soil. Then the wagons rolled on.

Ellis's grave became yesterday's memory, as had the Pawnee Fork and Walnut Creek. They toiled deeper into loneliness. They were in short-grass country now, and they met their first buffalo—scattered outriders of the great herds that were moving southward farther to the west.

Deer were plentiful in the river brush, and antelope bobbed on the swells. One morning Alex saw a wild horse herd running free and proud in the depths of the plains.

He was riding ahead, scouting the way with Zack Dixon. Behind them the wagons now traveled in compact formation—three abreast at the moment, though they swung into columns of fours when the trail permitted. The cordon of flankers had been doubled.

The marks of battle with Keno Dane were vanishing from Alex's face. His hands were almost normal again. He had seen Dane up and about two days after the fight. Except for scars the gunman, like Alex, seemed to have suffered no permanent damage.

Dane stayed carefully clear of Alex. And so did other members of Morgan Webb's fighting crew. And they had ceased their attempts to take over control of the caravan.

Morgan Webb had stated his views in the matter. "From what I saw, Alex Briscoe started the trouble by horning into a matter that was none of his affair," he said. "It's a personal affair between him and Dane. However, I hired Dane and these other men to guard us from Indian attack. I'm sure they'll earn their money if we're jumped. I have warned them not to hunt trouble with Briscoe or anyone else while they're in my pay. As long as Alex leaves Keno alone, I'm sure there will be no trouble."

Then Webb had added, "But I can't vouch for what will happen afterwards. It looks to me like Alex has earned himself a lot of grief."

Everyone knew Dane had suffered a hard blow to his reputation as a fighting man, and that the matter was not ended. There were even a few who hinted to Alex that it might be best for the peace of mind of everyone if he parted company with the caravan. These were the timorous ones who were also beginning to regret starting this journey in the face of the Indian threat.

Alex knew it would not take much to stampede some members of the company into turning back, even at this stage of the trip. If that started, it might panic the others.

He twisted in the saddle to gaze back. Len Capehart was riding as a flanker, first in line to the right. It was a position from which he could keep Alex in sight and protect him with his rifle. Since the night of the Keno Dane fight Capehart had never been far away from Alex, asleep or awake.

Alex had scoffed and pretended that he was being babied. Secretly he admitted that Capehart's vigilance was enormously comforting.

He kept telling himself that it was to Capehart's and Char Shannon's interests that he be kept alive until he had located the trail of the money shipment at least.

Still—he found himself wanting to find some conclusive

assurance that he was wrong about Capehart's having engineered the ambush of his wagons. In spite of his suspicions his respect for the Tennessean kept building in his mind.

On the other hand, Capehart's attitude had grown even cooler and more distant and distrustful toward him. Even though he was guarding Alex's life at Char Shannon's request, they seemed further apart than ever in the way of any mutual understanding.

Alex's gaze searched for Char, but she was riding in his moderately loaded wagon, which she used as a dressing room. She evidently was at siesta.

Capehart was swinging a light bullwhip with a ten-foot lash as he rode along, picking out brush or insects as his targets. The report of the popper was pungently sharp against the grinding rumble of the caravan.

Whip popping had become a standard source of amusement among the men of the company since Char had set the example. It helped relieve the tedium of a journey where time and distance was measured only by the number of revolutions a wagon wheel would make between sunrise and twilight.

Capehart uttered an exultant shout, and Alex saw him dragging at the end of the lash the wriggling length of a rattlesnake the neck of which he had snapped with the popper.

This was prairie dog country, a favorite place for rattlers. The reptiles were all too numerous in the grama and sage.

Capehart's feat brought Char into view in the wagon. She leaped to the ground, carrying a saddle, and rigged her mare, which was on a lead rope. Mounting, she hastened to join Capehart, a whip curled around her arm. Alex knew that she held a complete horror of rattlers and conducted a relentless campaign against them.

Alex straightened and stood in the stirrups. Teamsters and swampers all up and down the line were staring. He heard the rumble of startled comment.

For Char was violating another rule of decorum. Up to now she had bowed to custom and had mounted side saddle and suffered the discomfort of voluminous riding skirts.

This time she was astride. Worse yet, she had scorned to resort to the subterfuge that some women employed of wearing a flowing divided skirt to cover the fact that there were trousers beneath. Char had gone all the way. She was wearing breeches alone. And they fitted her slim figure to perfection.

She became aware of the sensation she was creating. She dismounted, bowed gracefully, sweeping her straw sombrero to the ground. She walked around, her hand on a hip in mincing scorn of their opinions.

Len Capehart, outraged, took direct action. He motioned to other flankers to close in. He left his position, angrily hurling his horse into a gallop, and descended on her. She was mounting the mare again, and was unaware of this danger.

"Makin' a show of yourself!" he yelled. "You need a tannin'!"

He was upon her before she could make a move to evade him. He plucked her bodily from the grulla mare and swung her across a knee. He attempted to spank that portion that was intended for spanking, and which was protected at this moment only by a tightened thin layer of the breeches she wore.

He landed one blow. Then Char exploded into wildcat fury. "You—you coward!" she panted. "Sneaking up on me when I wasn't looking!"

She twisted in his grasp and began beating at him with her hands and flailing with both legs. She was giggling hysterically, enjoying this.

The wagon train lurched to a stop. Men were holding their sides and rolling on the ground in the uninhibited, full-lunged merriment of the frontier.

Capehart was reaping the whirlwind. For self-protection he tried to wrap his arms around her in the hope of halting further danger from her churning arms and boots.

That maneuver unbalanced him. They both toppled from the saddle into the sagebrush, with Char still battling fiercely. They rolled over and over, with their horses nervously backing away.

Char screamed suddenly. Something in that sound brought sudden silence. There was no laughter, no lighthearted recklessness in that outcry. It was utter horror.

Alex raked his horse and sped toward them. She and Capehart had halted their personal struggle. They seemed to be crouching in arrested motion, staring at something.

Capehart moved. He snatched out a pistol and fired twice at an object in the sage at point-blank range.

Alex reached them and hit the ground running. Capehart was bending over Char, who had sunk back on the ground, her face ashen.

Nearby lay the quivering body of a diamondback rattlesnake.

Alex ripped the left sleeve of Char's calico blouse to the

shoulder and saw the fang marks just above the elbow.

"She took the strike in my place!" Capehart said, his voice thin and high with agonized self-reproach. "The snake sprang at my face as I lay on the ground. It would have got me, but she thrust her arm in front of me and it bit her instead."

Alex produced his hunting knife. He looked at her. "Hold onto something," he said. "I'm going to slash it so that we can suck out the poison."

"Slash away," Char said. Her lips were gray, but she was trying gamely to keep the stark fear out of her voice.

Alex drew the keen blade across the fang marks and blood ran. Capehart pushed him aside and drew the poison from the wound.

Alex, at the same time, tightened a tourniquet which he formed of his rolled neckerchief. "You're going to be all right," he told her. "We got to it fast, and that's what makes the difference."

"Lucky——" Char murmured faintly, the words coming now with an effort, for she was fighting faintness. "—lucky it wasn't my other arm. That's the one I need to pull on my britches. And roll cigarettes."

She wrinkled her nose at Capehart. "There's nothing I won't stoop to."

Then she passed out. Capehart was as pale as she. He looked at Alex, ran his tongue over his chalky lips, tried to say something—and failed.

The utter silence that had descended continued to hold as Alex lifted Char in his arms and carried her to the wagons.

Amelia appeared and offered the use of her vehicle. It was the first time since the night of Ellis's death that he had seen her. She had secluded herself back of the canvas curtains of her wagon.

She came to where he stood. She wore a dark, simple dress as an emblem of mourning, but was bareheaded. Once again she was her neat, composed self, a comely woman who seemed out of place in this rough trail life.

"I've been foolish and selfish, Alex," she said contritely. "In my affection for the dead I've forgotten my obligation to the living. I'll make amends. You must come and talk to me. I need someone who understands me."

She pressed his arm. Then she hurried away to help the other women with Char. She gave him a small and intimate smile over her shoulder. A promising smile.

Alex moved into the shade of a wagon and sat on a wheel hub, rolling one cigarette after another, waiting. But Capehart seemed oblivious of discomfort. He heel-squatted in the blazing sun, never taking his gaze from Amelia's wagon, where Char was making her fight.

At last Amelia parted the flap and alighted. She came to where Capehart and Alex waited. "It's still too soon to be absolutely sure, but I believe we got to it in time," she said. "You must have drawn out the greater part of the poison, Mr. Capehart. I'm convinced she'll be as good as new in a few days."

Capehart said shakily, "Thank the good Lord for His mercy."

Alex walked away, leaving him standing there, a tall and lonely figure, his hat in his hand.

The caravan surged into motion again, for water and a campsite were still hours ahead. Alex rode again to join Zack Dixon on pilot.

They mounted a long swell that overlooked a grassy basin. The Arkansas River shimmered half a mile to their left.

Directly before them lay something else—the wreckage of an arrow-skewered chuck wagon. The wind brought the harsh odor of putrefying flesh. There were dead horses scattered about the basin with more arrows jutting from their swollen bodies. But not all of this taint came from animals.

"Crew of Texas drovers," Zack Dixon said presently, the cold sweat standing out on his leathery forehead. "No sign of cattle. Looks like they were headin' for home with the chuck wagon after deliverin' a herd at Hays."

They found five mutilated bodies of men. The signs showed that they had been hit by a sizable party of Indians. More than fifty, Zack Dixon estimated.

" 'Rapahoes," he said. "It happened about two days ago."

Alex guided the caravan well away from this scene of carnage and led a burial party to the spot. He warned the men to minimize what they were to see.

But afterwards, when the wagons were in motion again, he saw the unmistakable signs of panic. News like that could not be kept secret. Everyone in the company knew what he and Zack Dixon had stumbled upon back there in that prairie swale.

Presently Amelia, mounted side saddle on one of Morgan Webb's blooded horses, rode out to join Alex. She wore a dark riding habit and English-style boots.

She ignored Joe Wallace's signals to stay with the wagons. "Mr. Wallace lets Char Shannon ride where she pleases," she said as she fought the nervous thoroughbred. "At any rate, I feel safer with you, Alex. A lot of the people are very frightened."

"We'll make Fort Dodge tomorrow," Alex said. "Maybe they'll settle down by that time."

"Some intend to demand a cavalry escort beyond Dodge," she said. "But Morgan says that's impossible, as the garrison at the fort is too small to spare men. Some of the immigrants and several owners of freight wagons also say they'll turn back to Hays City rather than cross the Arkansas without army protection."

She added, "But you can't afford to delay, Alex. I know why you are making this trip. It is easy to guess. What will you do if the others turn back?"

"Keep going," Alex said.

She placed her fingers on his gloved hand where it lay on the saddle horn. "Is it worth such a risk?" she asked, her voice sweetly concerned. "You said your wagons were lost beyond the Jornada. How far beyond?"

"Quite a ways," Alex said.

"I believe you mentioned that it happened at the upper spring of the Cimarron," she said. "Or did I get that mixed up with something else?"

"You likely did," Alex said easily.

She was nettled. "You think it is none of my concern, I see. I'm merely worried about you. Anyway, Len Capehart must have a pretty good idea of where it happened."

Alex sat a moment, organizing his thoughts. "I shouldn't have mentioned, even to you, that I suspected Capehart," he said. "Apparently he told the truth when he said some of his horses carrying the Shannon brand were stolen on the trail. A driver who is traveling with us right now was with Capehart on that trip from Santa Fe. I talked to him. He verified that Indians ran off some of their stock. Maybe those Indians were white men."

"Are you sure it isn't Char Shannon who has sweet-talked you into believing Capehart isn't as bad as you suspect?" she asked chidingly. She added, "Some women can twist you to their purpose too easily, Alex."

She turned her horse away then, saying she was tiring. She was angered by her failure to gain information from him. And her vanity was wounded. She had counted on her personal allure—and had learned nothing.

Returning to her wagon, she found Char looking better. She became very helpful and gracious.

After camp had been made that evening, Char, who was throwing off the effects of the snake bite, was moved into a tent which had been set up near the Shannon wagons.

Once she was alone Amelia got out a map of the trail and studied it. Her mention to Alex of the upper spring of the Cimarron as the place of the treasure had been a stab in the dark in an attempt to surprise him into talking.

Gazing at the great distances the map encompassed, she realized with finality that he alone held the secret of the bullion's location. The vast and broken country which lay around the camp at this very moment was only a sample of the harsher lands ahead.

She thought of the hazards that hung over Alex beyond the usual dangers of the trail. There was always the chance that the truce between him and Capehart might end at any moment. They were proud men, tempered to a fine edge. A wrong word, a wrong move by either might bring the flash of gunfire.

For, in addition to Alex's suspicion of Capehart in the matter of the wagon ambush, a new factor was adding tension between them. Amelia's feminine perception told her that back of this was that timeless element—a woman. That woman was Char Shannon.

And then there was Keno Dane. She knew Dane had stayed his vengeance on Alex only at Morgan Webb's insistence. Webb wanted Alex alive until he had revealed to Amelia the location of the wagon ambush. But Dane could not be restrained forever. He would kill from ambush sooner or later.

It occurred to her that Webb was now completely dependent on her ability to gain, by feminine wiles, the information he needed from Alex.

That aroused a new train of thought. She began to speculate on the possibility that she might possess all that treasure for herself alone if she played her cards adroitly.

She opened the leather trunk in which the bulk of her wardrobe was packed. She delved among the garments to the bottom, and her fingers caressed packets of money.

Twenty thousand dollars was stored there—the proceeds of Ellis Hartley's share of Alex's company. Ellis had insisted on bringing the cash with them, for he had held no intention of ever returning to Hays City. For the sake of easier transportation and lighter weight Amelia had converted the gold coin, which Char had paid her husband, into federal gold notes at a Hays City bank the day before the caravan's departure.

Amelia had often stroked those packets. The thought of such wealth had been very comforting. Now there was dissatisfaction in her. Twenty thousand dollars seemed insignificant.

"If I had all that bullion I'd really be rich," she breathed to herself. "Someday I might build it into a million. Two million. Then I'd wipe my slippers on Char Shannon."

14 ✶ IF THE Indians who had massacred the Texans were still east of Fort Dodge they avoided the big wagon train, for it arrived at the army post unchallenged. But there were some members who announced that they were withdrawing from the company and intended to head back to Hays. Others were dubious.

As soon as camp was settled, Morgan Webb prodded the fiddle player into sawing out a tune. "These people need to kick up their heels again," he said.

Amelia appeared, demurely becoming in a dark green wide-skirted dress, and with a tiny chip hat pinned on her glossy brown hair. Webb escorted her into the circle and they began dancing. The rest fell into the spirit of the thing. Fear thawed.

Officers from the fort arrived and joined in. Troopers watched from the background.

Char, who was now recovering rapidly, danced one turn around the circle with Zack Dixon, and then decided to sit out the rest of the evening.

"It's my first snake bite," she explained. "And I intend to wring all the sympathy possible out of my illness."

Alex noticed that Capehart stood in the background with the fixed look of a man suffering the torture of the damned.

Amelia abandoned her stiff formality and was the belle of the party. She danced with teamsters and with army officers without partiality. She even dragged Capehart into the circle and forced him to join her in a lively number.

After an hour Joe Wallace called a halt. "Save some o' that energy fer the trail," he said. "We'll need it when we hit the Arkansas an' find ourselves facin' the Jornada."

Capehart escorted Amelia to her wagon. Alex helped Char to the tent.

Capehart returned, drew his tobacco pouch from the breast

pocket of his shirt. As he did so an object fell to the ground at his feet.

Char picked it up. "Your watch, Len!" she exclaimed. "It may be broken!"

"Watch?" Capehart said. "I don't own a watch!"

Alex took the gold-backed timepiece from Char's hand. It was of expensive Swiss make, small and thin, but efficient. He gazed at it a moment, then handed it to Capehart.

"You should be more careful, Len," he said slowly. "That was no place to carry another man's watch."

He turned and walked away. Char came with a rush, overtaking him. She caught his arm and forced him to stand and face her.

"Tell me!" she demanded. "Tell me!"

Alex debated it a moment. "That watch belonged to Bill Stoker, a teamster who worked for me," he finally said. "In fact, my father gave it to Bill six or seven years ago after he had stood off Apaches who jumped our wagons on the Chihuahua trail."

"Go on," she said grimly.

"Bill Stoker was carrying that watch when he left Santa Fe with me. He was one of the three men who were murdered in the ambush. His body must have been searched for valuables before it was burned."

Char stood gazing at him, horror on her face. Then she turned and fled from him.

In her wagon Amelia turned down the wick in the lantern to a pale glow for the sake of modesty and prepared for bed. She drew back the coverlet on the pallet and removed her dress and the petticoats, and hung them neatly and carefully, pinning them in place in readiness for the jostling they would undergo as usual on the morrow.

She unlaced her small corset and drew air gratefully into her lungs. She admired her dim figure briefly in the mirror, then began working complexion compound into her face and hands.

She was at this task when fingernails scratched the wagon sheet. She pulled on a dressing gown and extinguished the lantern. She parted the rear canvas flap. Morgan Webb stood there. She seated herself just inside the wagon flap where she was concealed to her shoulders, and where she could whisper to him.

The moon laid a clear silver glow over the camp, but Webb hovered carefully in the shadow.

"It worked," he murmured. "I kept an eye on Capehart. Damned if he didn't drop that watch right at Alex Briscoe's feet. Alex recognized it. There was no doubt about that. He was wearing a scowl as black as thunder when he passed by me where I was watching from cover. That was a brilliant idea of mine, my dear, in starting that dance so you could have Capehart as a partner."

"On the contrary, it was a stupid blunder," Amelia said.

"Blunder? What do you mean?"

"It was entirely too obvious," Amelia said. "I realized it after it was too late. Alex Briscoe is no fool. Nor are Char Shannon and Len Capehart. They'll know that the watch was planted on him. They may suspect me."

She studied Webb intently. "You knew that, didn't you, and stampeded me into it with your fast talk," she said, a fury in her voice. "Why?"

Webb laughed. "Now that we understand each other, I'm sure you will destroy a certain letter you left with someone at Hays when you return there. If you agree, I'll also burn a letter of my own which I intend to mail at the fort in the morning. I will send it to my lawyer with instructions that it, like your letter, be opened only in case of my death. It will contain interesting reading."

"For instance?" Amelia asked grimly.

"It will tell about a girl who planted false evidence of murder on a man," Webb said.

"So that's the real reason you talked me into that idiotic thing?"

Webb laughed again. "Yes. My letter also will tell how a wife knew her husband had been shot because he was drinking too much, and was trying to tell things that had better be left unsaid. But she preferred to say nothing to the law about her knowledge. That is also a crime, my dear."

A bitter silence came. "Or am I offending your delicate sensibilities by mentioning these things?" Webb sighed.

"I, of course, would not trust you to carry out your part of the bargain," Amelia said. "As you are well aware."

"Strange," Webb said. "I was entertaining the same thought about you, my dear."

"Where did you get that watch?" she asked. "You weren't with Grassman when he—let us say—took over Alex Briscoe's wagons. You were in Hays, establishing your alibi."

"Grassman brought the watch to Hays," Webb explained. "I found it in his saddlebag after he was killed. He came first to my office, and the night hostler told him I had just left for Char Shannon's home. Grassman was the kind who couldn't resist stealing a watch, even though its possession would have put his neck in a noose."

"How did Grassman get to Hays?" she asked.

"The same way Alex did," Webb said. "He must have been left afoot when the Indians killed the rest of his bunch. He came into Hays mounted. His horse was a Texas cow pony and the rig was Tejano also. He must have stolen the horse, saddle and saddlebags, and all, from some trail men. Probably at Fort Dodge at about the same time Alex was borrowing one there. That's how they came to arrive at Hays the same night within an hour of each other."

He paused and added, "But we were discussing certain letters that are to be destroyed by agreement, my dear."

Amelia appraised him coolly. "I may marry you, Morgan," she said reflectively. "In fact, there was a time when I would have longed for such a thing."

"Marry me?" Webb was annoyed.

"A husband and wife cannot testify against each other," she pointed out. "Yes. I've decided on it. We will be married at Santa Fe—if you are still alive."

"Alive? Why won't I be alive?"

"The only reason Alex hasn't connected you with this affair is that he still does not know you were in Santa Fe at the time Grassman was given money to hire men to ambush the bullion wagons. He will find it out eventually, however."

"And you intend to tell him?" Webb demanded harshly.

"Hardly. But other persons must have seen you there. You could not have kept your presence entirely a secret. He'll learn this. Then all the loose ends will snap together in his mind."

She eyed him and went on, "Alex is a person who acts fast. Remember Grassman. He has been in his grave many days already."

Then she dropped the wagon flap, shutting her in. "Good night, Morgan," she said. "I'm going to bed now. I'm drowsy."

Webb heard her lash the canvas in place and sigh serenely as she lay down on the pallet. In a moment her soft, steady breathing told him that she was already asleep.

He walked away, a confused, baffled man. He was aware now that he was no longer his own master.

In the deep shadows of a wagon in the background Char Shannon also stirred presently and moved quietly away. Returning to her tent, a tall figure appeared at her side out of the darkness so silently that she broke off a gasping scream just in time. It was Capehart.

"I been worryin'," he said. "I found out you was missin' from your tepee, so I hung around."

"I've been doing some snooping," she whispered. "I—I've been keeping track of Amelia Thayer."

"And you found out something," he said. "What is it?"

"Amelia and Morg Webb had a powwow in the dark at her wagon," she murmured. "I was some distance away and had no idea what was said. It could have been harmless enough."

"Amelia planted that watch on me," Capehart said. "You know that too, don't you, Char?"

"But we're not sure," she said. "We only think she did it. And it's not what we believe that counts. It's what Alex Briscoe thinks. And—and he may be in love with Amelia. At least she acts like there is something between them."

She rushed into the small tent then, leaving Capehart there in the darkness. She undressed and turned in. But sleep would not come. She was still awake when a cracked bugle sounded the turnout call at first daybreak. Soon the wagons were in motion again.

15 ★ ALEX STOOD with Zack Dixon and Joe Wallace and other grim men, listening to the night. It was quiet—entirely too quiet.

The moon, past the full, rode the sky. Dawn was still more than an hour away, and a chill wind that came off the plains, always at this hour, stirred the duck saddle jacket Alex wore.

He had a rifle slung on his arm, and carried a brace of cap-and-ball pistols. A belt of rifle shells was hung over his shoulder, and the pockets of his jacket were heavy with spare cylinders for the pistols, primed and capped and loaded, and dipped lightly in melted beeswax to protect the charges.

The others were also armed to the teeth. A night bird whistled off to the west, the call thin and lonely. Another answered in the opposite direction. Presently an owl offered its harsh, grumbling plaint. An answer came from a distance.

"They're out there," Zack Dixon sighed. "Better rouse out

any thet are still asleep an' tell 'em to git ready. We're in fer it, for sure."

The wagons, interlocked in the frontier phalanx, cast soot-black shadows in the moonlight, and this glow painted their hoods to hammered silver. Nearby, the stock herd was held under doubled guard.

Well to the west the ragged outline of a low bluff formed a dim pattern against the sky, but in all other directions the stars came down to an unbroken horizon. However, there were coulees and breaks in these plains, and near at hand were gullies and swells which would give cover to a determined attacker.

This was the heart of the Jornada, so named by the early Spanish traders who had suffered and died on this waterless stretch of desolation between the Arkansas River and the course of the Cimarron. This was where entire caravans had lost their way and perished in sandstorms and northers.

This was the Jornada, across which the great buffalo herds grazed, and which the tribes—Cheyenne, Comanche, Arapahoe, Kiowan, Pawnee, and even the fierce Apache from the west and the mounted Ute from the north—regarded as their hunting ground.

Far behind now was Fort Dodge. Ten wagons had quit the journey there, but the remainder had forded the Arkansas at the point called the Middle Crossing by trail men.

The Cimarron was now little more than a day's march ahead at the slow pace the laden wagons traveled. They had camped at sundown, for Zack Dixon, scouting the trail, had sighted an enormous herd of migrating buffalo to the southwest. The animals were drifting eastward and would cross their route ahead.

They had decided it would be safer to wait until the following day to reach water at the Cimarron rather than risk being caught in a buffalo stampede.

A more urgent reason was that Dixon had also discovered that the country ahead was swarming with Indian hunting parties.

"They know we're here," he had said. "If we're in fer a fight, it'd be better to make our stand here where we're in the open an' kin handle the stock. We're nearin' broken country, an' they'd like nothin' better than to hit us when we was strung out over a rough trail. There's no use tryin' to turn tail an' run. They'd cut us to pieces all the way back to the Arkansas an' finish us as we bucked that quicksand."

The wagons had been interlocked in the defense phalanx and barricaded with barrels and cases of cargo. Men now moved through the camp awakening the sleepers to the freezing realization that Zack Dixon's fears were being fulfilled, and that they soon might be fighting for their lives. The camp was surrounded.

Alex went to Amelia's wagon and aroused her. He heard hysteria enter her voice when she comprehended the situation. She appeared from the wagon, partly dressed, her hair in disorder. She began to sob as he led her to where the women were assembling in a strong point that had been formed at the center of the wagon circle.

Char took Amelia off his hands. She wore man's garb, and so did the other women.

"We'll get Amelia dressed properly," she told him. "It'll be better if the Indians didn't know there are women with the outfit."

Len Capehart's tall form emerged from the darkness. "Good luck, Char," he said awkwardly.

She walked to him and kissed him on the mouth. She clung to him for a moment. "And good luck to you, Len," she said. "You know I believe in you."

Capehart turned and spoke suddenly, violently to Alex. "I never saw that watch in my life before it dropped from my pocket there at the fort that night," he burst out. "And if you don't want to believe that, then to hell with you."

He stalked away, his rifle on his arm. It was the first time he had permitted his pride to bend far enough even to mention the matter of the murdered Bill Stoker's watch to anyone.

Alex and Char looked at each other uneasily. Then Alex hurried away to help with the stock.

The bells on the herd leaders were muffled, and the animals were hazed into a rope corral that had been formed against the wagon circle.

"If'n them hawsses an' mules stampede they'll kill as many as the injuns," Zack Dixon prophesied gloomily.

Silence came again. Alex gazed at the eastern horizon. The morning star was beginning to blaze, and the moon had lost its glitter.

He moved along the line of barricaded wagons and found a firing position and settled down, laying out his ammunition so that it would be within quick reach.

Len Capehart moved in just to his left. Alex smiled grimly. He had expected that. Even now Capehart meant to stand vigil over him.

Char came crawling in between them and pushed a rifle across a wagon box. She had left the safer central shelter and moved into the fighting line. "I'm scared," she said.

Slowly, inexorably all the sterile hills and the swells with their woolly cover of buffalo grass emerged from night's shadows as though the land were rising from a black sea.

Then Zack Dixon's voice rose. "Here they come!"

The gray land, which had lain so lifeless beneath a sky that was gaining the rose-and-pink flush of a new day, spewed forth a screaming mass of Indians.

Rifles on both sides began their roaring. Arrows were hissing and spears were flashing, and both white men and red men were screeching—and dying.

Alex fired at those indistinct figures that flitted and darted before his sights. He kept shouting at Char, "Be careful! Be careful! Stay down! Stay down!"

And all the time he was aware that she was screaming and shooting, just as he was yelling and shooting.

This was the frenzy of battle that now held all of them.

The Indians in the first wave of the attack were on foot. Alex identified them. Cheyennes and Arapahoes.

Now the roar of hooves arose, and a long line of mounted Indians swept over the crest of a rise to the west, and came at the wagons in a thunderous charge. They carried shields of buffalo hide and long lances. These mounted warriors were Comanches, Alex saw. And Kiowas.

The wagon train was confronted by a coalition. All the tribes seemed to have united for this fight. Alex heard the shrilling of whistles through the tumult. Pawnees.

Indians, both on foot and mounted, were at the wagons now, and some were inside the circle, fighting hand to hand.

Alex emptied his rifle. He stood with revolvers exploding, firing at figures that were painted and at faces that were wild and savage. Then these guns went empty also, and he had no chance to reload.

He fought with his hands, swinging the rifle. To his right he saw Char striking frantically at a warrior who had seized her by her hair.

Before Alex could move to help her, Capehart had turned and fired, killing the Indian.

Alex felt the thirsty graze of an arrow on his shoulder. A thrown lance tore his hat from his head.

He found a chance to push new loaded cylinders into his pistols and began shooting again, clearing away the space around them.

Then no more Indians were coming at them. Elsewhere the attack had recoiled also, withering under the gunfire that kept gusting from the wagons. The warriors who had fought their way into the circle had been wiped out.

A general retreat started. The Indians ran and rode away, carrying dead and wounded with them.

Wagon men staggered and fell to the ground, retching, their lungs tortured beyond endurance, their muscles numb and knotted from the terrible exertion of the fight.

Dead and wounded men, both defenders and attackers, lay around the wagons. An immigrant's wife ran wildly from one form to another until she found her husband. He was dead, and she began weeping, and rocking back and forth in grief.

Char was leaning against a wheel, looking around with a blank, stunned expression. She slid limply to the ground, sitting there wanly, all the starch gone out of her.

Capehart was nursing a livid welt on his forehead. "War club," he mumbled. "Saw it comin'. Couldn't duck in time. But I got a thick skull. I'm all right."

Alex carried Char to the central barricade despite her protests that she was able to travel on her own feet.

"I'm sorry I got swoony," she said.

She was shaking off the terror now. Wounded were being brought to the inner barricade, and she began helping other wagon people in caring for them.

Amelia crouched in a corner, chattering hysterically. Char walked to her and said, "This is for your own good, Amelia. We need help now—not theatrics."

And she slapped Amelia sharply on the cheek, drew back her hand, and slapped her again.

Amelia's sobs ended instantly. She stared up at Char, a dull, sullen rage replacing the glazed terror in her eyes.

"That's better," Char said.

She took Amelia's hand comfortingly. "It was the only way, Amelia," she said. "Now, stay here with me. I'll tell you what to do."

Warning shouts ran around the circle. The Indians had reorganized, and were mounting a new attack.

Alex had shattered the stock of his rifle during the first fight. He hastily searched and found a Henry rifle that had belonged to a man now dead and rejoined Capehart at the barricades.

Char scrambled into position, a rifle in her hand. Even the wife who had been mourning her husband seized up a gun and took her place in the firing line.

98

Dust and powder smoke from the first melee still hung low over the camp in the windless morning.

Then came the Indians. This second charge was pressed with greater determination than the first. And it was resisted even more fiercely.

Alex found himself standing back to back with Capehart above Char, battling with warriors who swarmed over the barricade. He shot an Indian who had been about to brain Capehart with an ax.

As he was warding off a blow from another warrior, an Indian leaped on his back. He knew that he would have died then, but for Char, who fired point-blank into the body of this assailant. The bullet killed the Indian as he tried to plunge a knife into Alex's throat.

It was a fantasy of painted faces and smoke and blood, and the screams of the injured and the shouts of the combatants.

It went on and on, and Alex fought with no hope of emerging alive. Then the terrible tide receded suddenly, just as it had before. The Indians, their guns empty, their losses heavy, had wavered again just at the moment when complete victory might have been theirs. Once more they were fleeing away through the battle smoke.

Alex clung to a wagon until his legs steadied and his heart eased its hammering. Capehart, his shirt partly torn away, sat gasping. He had a knife slash across his ribs, but Alex saw that it was not deep.

Char also seemed to have escaped damage. She crouched, gazing around as though unable to believe they were still alive.

Alex discovered that his left arm was numb from a blow from some weapon, but the bone appeared intact. There were bullet burns on him, and bruises whose source he could not remember. Death had missed him many times by only inches—as it had the others.

He saw Keno Dane walking through the scene of carnage, a revolver in each hand, his teeth showing in a pleased smile. Alex remembered having seen Dane crouching at a strong point with that same look on his face, his guns blazing as he took savage toll. Evidently, for once, Dane had been furnished with enough targets to satisfy his lust for killing.

A wagon was burning, and the flames now spread to other vehicles, threatening the destruction of the caravan.

Horses and mules that had broken their hobbles were stampeding about, frenzied by the smoke and flames and confusion. Alex saw Joe Wallace lying dead beside one of the burning wagons.

Alex organized a fire brigade, and they rolled the burning wagons out of line and moved the other vehicles into position to close the gaps in the circle.

Meanwhile Capehart saw to it that the wounded were cared for and preparations made to bury the dead. There were ten slain wagon people. Double that number bore serious wounds, but there were half a dozen of these who might be able to handle a gun if necessary.

They still had a fair supply of rifles and ammunition. The caravan could muster nearly seventy able persons on the firing line.

"There must be three, four hundred warriors out there," Zack Dixon said. "They aim to finish the job."

It was evident now that it was to be a siege. The main body of Indian allies had withdrawn out of rifle range, but the dry stream bed north of the circle was occupied by Comanches and Kiowas with rifles and arrows. And there were other positions behind swells and outcrops which warriors reached by wriggling in on their stomachs, following every contour of the land.

From these points came a nagging fire as the sun climbed higher and the morning wore along. Horses were being hit—and occasionally a human.

Alex looked in on the inner barricade. Char and the other women were working steadily to ease the suffering of injured, but Amelia had given up again. She sat slumped in a corner on a buffalo robe, her face buried in her hands.

Alex returned to his fire fighting. They had little water to spare, but were forced to use some of the supply to soak blankets, for fire arrows were being used by Indians hidden in gullies.

16 ★ NOON CAME, and the coolness of dawn was only a memory. The naked iron hoops of the fire-blackened wagons stood hot and gaunt against a glaring sky in which floated a molten yellow sun. Buffalo gnats and flies swarmed around the hospital area.

Capehart placed an armed guard over the water supply, for

Keno Dane and his men had been helping themselves as they pleased.

Morgan Webb appeared. It was the first time Alex had noticed him all day. He surmised that Webb had stayed clear of the worst of the fighting. The yellow-haired man carried a silver-mounted rifle and holstered six-shooters with carved grips.

He had Keno Dane at his side. He hunted up Alex and Capehart.

"You men seem to have taken charge, now that Joe Wallace is dead," he said. "Your authority is questionable because it is a matter the entire company should have been asked to vote on. However, as long as you have assumed the responsibility, we would like to know what your plans are for getting us out of this mess."

"Outlast 'em," Alex said. "There's no other way."

"Outlast them?" Webb exploded. "Ridiculous! We're alrealy short of water!"

"So are they."

"But they can replenish theirs," Webb snapped. "They have access to the river."

"But every hour they spend here fighting us might bring them that much nearer to starvation next winter, and they know it," Alex said. "They're here to make meat and make robes. Instead, they've lost a lot of warriors, wasted valuable ammunition, and used up their horses. They may decide to see it through to a finish. If so, they'll probably wipe us out. But they may realize it isn't worth the cost and will pull out and follow the buffalo again. Perhaps we can prod them along in that decision."

"How?"

"We'll let you know if we need your help, Morg."

Webb lighted a cigar, inspected Alex carefully through the first puff of smoke, then walked away dissatisfied.

"My medicine tells me his gun slingers will light a shuck out of here to save their own hair if they get a chance," Capehart murmured. "And Morg with 'em. Did you really have anything in mind?"

"A while ago when I was on top of a wagon I had a look-see around," Alex said. "The country drops away southeast of here. I sighted at least two Indian camps about three miles away in that direction. They've moved in from the Cimarron to be close to the fight. There weren't many tepees, but it looked like there were squaws along. I could see frames for drying jerky. They figure on making meat at the same time they're taking care of us. And there were big herds of ponies on graze."

He looked at Zack Dixon. "And that big herd of buffalo that you sighted has slowed up. It's still west and south of us. It's grazing east, almost toward us—but surely toward the Indian camps. I took a look a little later and made sure of that. What we can do before the Indians decide to move camp tomorrow out of the path of the herd is to go out there after dark and——"

"I'm way ahead of you," Capehart said, his eyes lighting. "How far away do you figure the buffalo are right now?"

"Five, six miles," Alex said. "They'll be closer by dark."

An arrow buzzed through the air, buried its barbed head in the earth at Alex's feet. A bullet ripped a wide furrow in the weather-sagged brim of Capehart's hat. They leaped aside, realizing they had come under the observation of Indians who must have worked their way to a new firing point.

Thus it went during the afternoon. Two more mules were hit. A man sleeping in a barricade, apparently safe, was killed when an arrow ricocheted from a wheel hub. Two men fighting fires were wounded. More horses and mules were struck down.

Death was always at their elbow. Amelia became hysterical again until Char Shannon gave her a laudanum pill. Two wounded men were also showing signs of giving way to terror. The wounded feared they might be abandoned if the others decided to make a run for it.

Morgan Webb and Keno Dane and their crew had remained in a compact group all during the afternoon, staying hunkered deep behind the barricades.

Len Capehart knocked one of the surly gunmen senseless with a blow from the muzzle of his pistol when the man attempted, by force, to help himself to more than the water ration that had been established.

This man, it was evident to Alex, was near a crack-up. He was a short, thick-necked, underslung ruffian who went by the name of Gratt Garvey. Each time an arrow or a bullet tore through the wagons, Gratt Garvey cringed and tried to make himself smaller. Once, when a man was struck in the throat by an arrow and killed instantly, Garvey came to his feet with a choked yell of terror. He rushed upon Alex in a frenzy.

"We got to git out o' this trap!" he screeched. "They'll kill us all, one by one. Why don't you do somethin'?"

102

Alex and others prevailed on him to return to his hiding place. Keno Dane and his companions did not offer to help soothe their companion. They looked on with the indifference of men who have only contempt for weakness.

Mounted Cheyennes made a noisy and wild attack just at deep dusk. But it was not pressed vigorously. It was intended only to emphasize the terror of the siege. Whooping riders circled the wagons, hanging to the off side of their ponies while they displayed their skill at firing rifles and arrows from that position. When bullets from the barricades began to pick off ponies, the Cheyennes withdrew.

And so dusk came, with the hulks of the burned wagons still smoldering beyond the barricades and laying a repugnant odor of burning cloth from the bolts of calico and twill that had been among the contents.

Hot and tense darkness moved in, marked by the firefly flight of burning arrows.

A man came searching for Zack Dixon. "A feller jest tuk French leave of us," he reported. "He slipped past the barricades when nobody was lookin' an' went crawlin' off through the darkness. It was the one thet Len slapped around today at the water barrels. Gratt Garvey. Seems like he aims to weasel past the Injuns an' save his scalp by headin' back to Fort Dodge on foot. I could have shot him, for it was desertion, but couldn't bring myself to it."

Alex and Dixon walked to the north side of the circle and peered. No sound came from the darkness. If Gratt Garvey was still out there he had not been discovered.

"Maybe he got through," Alex said.

Other men had gathered around. Alex made out the bony face of Keno Dane among them. He believed he saw envy in the man's attitude. Dane evidently was wishing he had the courage to follow Garvey's example and try to escape from this deadly circle.

Then—some distance out from the wagons in the direction Garvey had been heading—a commotion arose. An Indian screeched. Garvey yelled in horror. The scuffling sound of a hand-to-hand fight could be heard.

The thud of a blow drifted to them. Garvey's voice arose begging for his life. The impact of another blow was sharp and ugly in the night.

Alex and the others stood rigid, listening. Presently an Indian began shouting. He taunted the wagon people in scornful Spanish.

"Do you make out what he's sayin'?" a man asked Alex.

"Maybe it would be better if I couldn't," Alex said. "That's a Comanche sub-chief who says his name is Hawk Feather who's doing the talking. He tells us they've got the white man, and will soon show us what will happen to all of us at their hands."

The silence descended again. It went on and on. Then a sound arose that silenced every movement in the wagon camp. Alex felt a freezing sickness rush through him. That wailing, sobbing voice was of a man in torture. It was the voice of Gratt Garvey—still alive!

Horror and panicky terror swept the camp. Amelia touched it off by screaming in utter fear.

A man began running in an aimless stampede. "Let's git out o' here!" he kept yelling in a hoarse voice. "Let's——"

Alex overtook him, caught him by the shoulder, and sent him spinning beneath a wagon with a blow from his fist.

Capehart moved in also, his two pistols in his hands. "Quiet everybody!" he ordered. "Don't give those warriors the satisfaction of knowing you're scared. That's what they want."

A red glow arose from the gully north of the camp. The Indians had ignited a fire there.

Something was lifted into view. Gratt Garvey again began screaming in agony. He had been lashed to a framework of lances and was suspended above the fire, to die in torture before the eyes of the wagon people.

The screaming went on and on. Alex tried to close his mind to it. He saw the putty-hued faces of the others.

He walked to the hospital barricade and looked in. Char was dressing the wound of an injured man and, with ashen face, was trying to ignore the terrible sounds in the night.

She finished her task. Suddenly she sprang to her feet and rushed to Alex. Throwing her arms about him, she clung tightly to him like a little child, burying her face against him while she shuddered and wept.

After a time she calmed and drew away from him. "I'm sorry," she said. She turned and went back to helping the wounded.

Presently the sounds out there faded and finally died. Garvey's ordeal was over—forever. The frame was lowered. Wild screeching began as the Indians began taking coup in the darkness.

Finally complete silence came once again.

Alex went to his wagon, delved into his war sack, and

changed to black breeches, a dark shirt, and an old pair of moccasins which he wore when stalking game.

He found charcoal in the ashes of a dead cook fire and began blackening his face and hands.

Capehart joined him, similarly garbed, and rubbed soot into his own skin.

Alex looked at him. "I was figuring on handling this thing by myself."

"Figure again," Capehart said. "I'm going with you."

Zack Dixon had discovered this unusual activity and was watching questioningly.

Alex looked at the plainsman. "What's the best way to stampede buffalo, Zack?" he asked.

Zack's old eyes lighted. "So that's it? Well, it might git us out of this fight at that. As fer startin' 'em runnin', you never know. Sometimes you can't budge 'em off'n a bedground, come hell an' hurricanes. Other times they'll skitter if you sneeze, an' run ten miles."

He added thoughtfully, "There's one thing all horned wild critters are scared of above all, an' that's the smell of burnin' hair. I'll hunt you up some old buffalo robes. They burn real good, an' we'll doctor 'em with grease and gunpowder to help out. If thet don't start 'em rollin', nothin' will."

"They're headed east, and if we can get them running they should take off in that direction," Alex said. "I'm hoping they'll run right over those Indian villages. If we can smash their supplies, scatter their ponies, and spook the buffalo out of the country the tribes will have something more important to think about than taking our scalps. But that appears to be a mighty big bunch of buffalo. A lot of 'em might come in this direction."

"We'll arrange to fix up a blockade of wagons an' I'll git some stuff ready to set afire," Zack said. "That'll split 'em past us. But it ain't the stampede I'm frettin' about. We'll cross that river when we git to it. There's somethin' else to worry about first."

He paused and finally said reluctantly, "You just saw what happened to one feller who tried to sneak past them Injuns. The next ones won't be let off even as easy as he was."

Nobody wanted to comment on that. Alex said to Capehart, "Ready?"

Amelia came rushing into the circle. She kissed Capehart, then clung to Alex, kissing him repeatedly. "You'll get us out of this awful place, won't you?" she wept.

Char stood in the background, her eyes dark and brooding against the gray weariness of her face. She looked at Capehart, then at Alex. "I'll pray," she said. "Be careful. Both of you."

17 ★ ALEX LED the way as they slid over the barricades and wormed away from the wagons into the darkness. Capehart stayed some half a dozen yards back. Moonrise was still more than an hour away, but the stars blazed down upon them and it did not seem to Alex they could hope to escape detection in that brilliance. Yet he knew that this was an illusion, for he could not see even the hummocks of grass and brush until they were only little more than arm's length away.

The buffalo grass, clinging close to the earth, was dry and cured, so that each hand, each knee, had to be eased down with breathless caution to avoid any betraying rustle. There were patches of sage and small brush—and gullies where pebbles were loose.

Each tiny sound was like an explosion on their taut nerves. Time after time Alex mistook tufts of bunch grass for a waiting Indian in the starlight.

Each carried a knife and a pistol and had buffalo robes strapped on his back. In addition Capehart had found a horsehair-stuffed pillow on a wagon and had appropriated it.

Alex inched ahead. Slowly the wagons fell astern and were lost in the darkness. They were moving westward, in the hope the Indians would least expect a breakout in that direction.

The occasional scuttle of some small animal or lizard would freeze them into immobility for seconds until they were sure of the source. Once, a rattlesnake aroused almost beneath Alex's groping hand. It buzzed briefly, then glided away, and he could hear the rattles clicking gently. He had to wait for a time until his heart returned to normal.

As they advanced farther, sounds came to them that were not made by reptiles. A lone Indian walked past within a dozen yards of them, so close that he loomed up against the stars as Alex lay flat, peering, his knife ready in his hand.

They waited a long time, then moved ahead again. Soon the peculiar, wild, smoky smell of Indians became strong, and Alex guessed that a number of warriors must be sleeping nearby.

They passed this danger also without stirring alarm. Pallor on the horizon warned that moonrise was near. Alex made out a low bluff ahead in the darkness and recognized it. They were nearly a mile from the wagons. That meant they probably were beyond the Indian lines.

They proceeded with caution for another quarter of an hour, then mounted the bluff. They traveled at a half trot.

The wild and earthy odor of buffalo came on the wind. An animal snorted and moved out of their path. The moon was lifting above the swells now, and they could make out more buffalo ahead. They were on the outskirts of the great herd.

They worked their way farther west, circling scattered bands and lone animals that were bedded away from the main body. The buffalo had not learned to fear men on foot. Even so, an uneasiness began to spread among them as Alex and Capehart moved ahead.

They had hoped to gain the far fringe of the herd before attempting to stampede the animals, but there seemed to be no limit to the size of this assemblage.

"It's no use," Alex finally said. "It's near midnight already, by the way the stars swing. This bunch might stretch for miles more. There's no telling. We'll have to try it now. The buffalo that are up are grazing east, and that's the right direction for us."

They searched around until they found a small outcrop of rock that lifted some twenty feet to its apex above the grassy plain. It would offer a haven.

They got out matches and moved among the buffalo, spreading the horsehair from the pillow, and placing the robes, and sprinkling gunpowder.

They touched off the blaze and raced toward the rocks. The gunpowder flashed into smoky, noisy flames. All the buffalo in the vicinity broke into retreat from this surprising thing. But it was not a stampede, merely a shifting away from something unknown.

Then the wind picked up the scent of burning hair and carried it to the herd.

That, too, was like touching flame to gunpowder. In the next instant every buffalo in the vicinity was running. The panic spread in a great tidal wave. Alex could hear the roar of hooves race in a wave of tumult far across the plain in the darkness.

The entire herd was stampeding now, rolling eastward toward the wagon circle and also toward the Indian camps.

Alex was fifty yards from the rocks, with buffalo bearing down on him when he stumbled over some obstacle and hit the ground in a breath-taking fall.

Capehart had been two strides ahead, his long legs carrying him over the ground swiftly, but he sensed disaster and turned. He snatched Alex to his feet and dragged him along at a stumbling run.

A bull buffalo came out of the moonlight at full speed, knocking them down. Other animals leaped over them without touching them. They got to their feet again. More buffalo were bearing down on them, but this time they made it to the shelter of the rocks.

They climbed as high as possible, then lay there panting. The outcrop was a tiny island amid a black, roaring flood, and it stood barely above the surface. The moon reflected on horns and gave glimpses of shining eyes.

The stampede was a titantic thing. The black tide extended southward as far as Alex could see in the moonlight. Dust was rising now, and beginning to obscure the scene. But the tumult went on and on.

There was no question but that the stampede was rolling upon the Indian camps, and also upon the barricaded wagons. Eastward they made out a red glow and knew the wagon people had touched off fires to split the herd.

Finally the last of the running animals were past. The roar deepened to a vast rumble in the night and that dwindled to a distant and echoing sound. The silence of the plains moved in again.

Alex thought of the moment when he was down and shaken, and of Capehart's readiness to help him.

He asked curiously, "Why did you do it?"

Capehart did not answer for so long that Alex decided his question was being ignored.

Then the Tennessean spoke. "I don't rightly know if I did it for you, Briscoe, or—for Char Shannon."

"For Char Shannon?"

"She don't deserve to be hurt by you, Briscoe."

"Hurt!" Alex exclaimed. "What are you trying to say?"

There was cold rage in Capehart's voice. "What is Amelia Thayer to you, Briscoe? What kind of a man are you? Char believes in you. She's—she's even falling in love with you."

"So that's what's in your craw?" Alex said.

108

"That's it," Capehart snapped. "If you're anything to Amelia Thayer, then stay away from Char Shannon. If she suffers any regrets from havin' trusted you, then you'll answer to me for it. With a gun!"

"Char Shannon doesn't need any man to defend her," Alex said. "As for being in love with me, you couldn't be farther wrong. The real truth is that I'm her only hope of keeping her freighting outfit in business. I'm valuable to her only as long as I have a chance of recovering that bullion. Speaking of that, who do you think planted Bill Stoker's watch on you that night?"

The sudden change of subject surprised Capehart. "Why, I figured you took that as final proof that I was mixed up in that business."

"You may be a fool where women are concerned," Alex said, "but you wouldn't be idiot enough to carry evidence like that around with you. And certainly not in a pocket where you'd be sure to drag it out with your tobacco. The watch was planted on you, of course. Who do you suspect?"

Capehart started to speak, then went silent for a time. "I'll let you know when I'm positive sure certain," he finally said. "There's been too much misunderstanding between folks already. Does this mean you no longer believe I had any hand in shootin' up your wagons an' stealin' that jag of treasure?"

"I don't imagine that a man who was guilty of that would have bothered to drag me out from under the stampede a few minutes ago," Alex said. "And you've had other chances to cash in my chips for me, but passed them up."

"Maybe, like Char Shannon, I'm only waitin' around until you lead us to the treasure," Capehart said.

"Like Keno Dane, you mean," Alex said quietly.

Capehart was silent a moment. "So you're wonderin' too why Dane hasn't tried to settle for that beatin' you gave him. Maybe he hasn't seen a chance when the break would be in his favor."

"And maybe he's got his orders," Alex said.

"Do you care to mention any names?"

"Morg Webb," Alex said tersely. "I've begun to take a look at him from a different slant. I thought he was only a big, pleasant voice that covered up a lot of nothing. I was mistaken—plenty. He's out to rake in the whole pot. He's winging around like a buzzard, waiting for Shannon Southwestern and Briscoe & Company to die, so that he can pick up the bones. That's why he hired Dane and that crowd of gunslicks. It proves that you can't read a man's mind by the way his hair is parted."

"Nor a woman's," Capehart said. "But how would Morg know about that stolen treasure?"

"I have only a hunch," Alex said slowly. "But my hunch about you was dead-wrong. This one may be also."

They fell silent. The exhaustion of the long day of battle bore down on them now, and suddenly they slept with that heavy dreamlessness of men who are utterly spent. Around them the last hours of the night passed, and a new day dawned in the sky.

They aroused and waited, watching, straining their eyes as daylight strengthened.

Abruptly visibility seemed limitless. The plains lay before them sharp and clear in this liquid light.

Except for the battle-blackened circle of wagons which was distinct some three or four miles away, and a far, far line of moving dots that were Indians riding over the horizon to the southeast, the land was utterly empty.

The buffalo were gone over the rim of the plains, and from this distance it was impossible to tell exactly where the Indian camps had stood, for the stampede had obliterated them.

The great herds of ponies which had grazed near the villages apparently had been swept away with the whirlwind, along with the squaws and the warriors.

All the signs of the carnage and the violence that had swirled around the wagon train the previous day were lost in the immensity of the land. The supreme indifference had returned to the face of the plains.

Those dots to the southeast—one of the scattered bands of Indians riding to overtake the buffalo or to round up their ponies—were now swallowed also by the blue haze of distance.

It was as though the last actors in a mighty drama had moved off into the wings, leaving the stage bare and waiting for the next act.

Capehart said, "Look! Even the wagons are fixin' to pull out! They're desertin' us!"

They began hurrying, but it was an hour before they topped the last rise and came into close view of the camp.

A dozen wagons were already on the move—heading north over the back trail toward the Arkansas River. Teams were hooked to the remaining vehicles, with the exception of the five owned by Alex and Char Shannon.

Char, backed by Zack Dixon, stood amid a group of men. It was evident a fierce dispute was in progress. Char had a six-shooter in her hand, and Dixon had his rifle slung at the ready in his arm.

All faces turned as they were sighted. Char came racing toward them.

"Thank heaven!" she choked. "You're—you're both alive!"

She flung her arms around Capehart and kissed him with fierce joy. She was laughing, but tears were flowing. "You need a shave, Len," she babbled in an attempt to cover her real emotions. "Kissing you is like falling on a bunch of cactus. I hope I don't have to speak to you about this again."

She turned and looked at Alex, a light in her eyes he again could not interpret. "I'm—I'm very glad," she said. "Very glad."

He eyed Zack Dixon questioningly. The plainsman shrugged. "You got Char to thank for findin' anybody still here," he said. "The company voted to turn back an' try to make it to Fort Dodge. But Char allowed that she wasn't leavin' until she was danged sure whether you two were dead or alive. An' she was persuadin' some others to stay. A six-gun in the hands of an angry gal is a mighty good persuader."

"This was before I realized what disreputable-looking persons they were," Char said. "In addition to whiskers they're covered with soot and dust. Whatever I found in them to worry about is more than I can understand."

"She said that if we had an ounce o' sand in our gizzards we'd go out there an' try to find you two ugly cusses," Zack grinned. "She seemed to be all upset about whether you was maybe lyin' wounded an' starvin' out there on this desert. This double-damned desert, she called it."

Zack continued to grin into his beard. "I promised her I'd personally find you if she'd only go along with the other wagons where they'd be safe. Damned if'n she'd stir a step. She allowed she'd shoot anybody who tried to lay a hand on her. She meant it, too. She sure did."

"It seems like some didn't wait," Capehart said, indicating the wagons that were traveling northward.

"They're jest a leetle more scared than the rest." Zack shrugged. "They're makin' tracks for Fort Dodge. They figure they might bump into more war parties if they kept goin' toward Santa Fe, an' that they was lucky to get out o' yesterday's scrape as easy as they did."

Alex waited, sensing that something more was to be explained.

Zack Dixon said, "It's Webb an' his men that are missin', if that's what you're wonderin'."

"Missing?"

"They ain't exactly missin'. Morg an' Keno Dane an' their gun guards lit a shuck out last night without any announcement right after the stampede went by. They tuk one wagon, but Morg's other wagons air still here. His men were a mite worked up, figgerin' he deserted 'em in order to make sure of his own scalp. They're likely well on their way to the Arkansas by now. They was travelin' light."

Then Dixon added casually, "Mrs. Thayer decided to go along with them."

Alex turned. "With them?"

"She was worried about her scalp too, I reckon," Zack explained. "She left it up to us to get her wagon back to Dodge."

Alex felt no surprise. He stood thinking, no emotion in his soot-blackened face. The strain of the past days had further leaned him, so that the heavy gun belt seemed to cut into his waist.

Like Capehart, he was gray with alkali. A blood-smeared neckerchief was wrapped around his left wrist, where a small wound he had received during the Indian fight had been reopened when he crawled through the brush. The marks of his battle with Keno Dane were still on his face.

Char Shannon misinterpreted his expression. "Amelia thought you were dead," she said hastily. "Otherwise she would have stayed."

Alex looked at her. "No," he said. "Not Amelia."

Zack Dixon spoke again. "It was Webb quittin' us that decided the others. Everybody forgot they owed it to you two to find out what had happened to you after the way you got us out of that Indian trap."

"Wal, Briscoe an' Capehart are here now, an' alive," a wagon owner snapped. "An' I'm rollin' north. My hair's gittin' mighty thin but I hope to hold onto what's left for a few years longer."

Whips began cracking in nervous haste. Dry wheel hubs creaked complainingly as teams snatched the wagons into motion. It was another stampede—a human stampede this time, back to safer country beyond the Arkansas River.

The Briscoe & Shannon crew men waited anxiously beside their wagons. Capehart looked at Char and Alex and then nodded. "Four or five wagons wouldn't have much chance if you were jumped, boys," he said. "Better string along with the rest of 'em and pull out for the Arkansas. You'll be safer in that direction."

Alex looked at Char. "You can either wait at the fort for word from me or go back to Hays," he said. "You'd be more comfortable at Hays."

"And you?" Char asked.

"I'm taking my wagon south," Alex said. "I'll stay under cover and travel at night as much as possible. One wagon is easier to hide than a string. If things work out, I'll be heading north again inside of three or four days."

"And if things don't work out?"

Capehart spoke. "We'll untangle that knot after it's tied, Char."

Alex looked at him. "This one might be a little tougher to figure out than that one last night. Are you sure you want to count yourself in again?"

Capehart gave him a thin smile. "Positive certain."

"But——!" Char began argumentatively. Then she realized the futility of opposing them.

"I'll wait at Fort Dodge," she said reluctantly. She added shakily, "I'll wait a long time."

Wagons were already heaving into motion. Stock losses had been heavy during the Indian fight, and Alex saw that many teams were short of their original strength.

He found that five of his duns had survived. These animals seemed to be in good shape, however, and he and Capehart felt they would be adequate.

They hooked the animals to the twelve-foot wagon, placing the odd horse as spike leader in the team. Char's mare had escaped injury, and Alex rigged it and helped her mount.

He stood for a moment at her stirrup. Keeping his voice down so that only she could hear, he said, "We're heading for a place about ten miles down the river from the middle springs of the Cimarron. That's where Grassman and his crowd burned the first wagon. From that point I hope I can pick up the trail of the wagon they used to haul the treasure away, and trace it to where they bumped into the Indians."

Char gazed at him a shining light in her eyes. "So you've decided that it's safe to trust a Shannon with that information?"

"Don't rub salt in an old wound," he said.

She laid a hand on his. "Luck," she said. "All the luck in the world."

She turned to Capehart, and her voice was a little shaky. "And wash your face, Len," she said.

She wheeled her mount and rode off to overtake the wagons. She did not look back. Capehart stood watching her, an empty and wistful mood draining all expression out of his face. "Let's dust off," he said. "We've got to make the Cimarron fast. Among other things we're out of is water."

Capehart mounted the near wheeler. Alex climbed into the wagon which had been emptied during the Indian fight of its pseudo cargo. The cases and barrels had been used to build the barricades.

Inside the wagon was a supply of food, along with cooking utensils and blankets, and a case containing new Henry rifles and two pistols and a plentiful supply of ammunition.

There were also fresh, clean bandages, and a medicine kit, and a bottle of brandy, along with a note written in Char's clear hand which admonished them not to neglect their injuries.

Char, Alex reflected, evidently never had permitted herself to doubt that he and Capehart would return alive from that mission to stampede the buffalo herd. And she had known they would go on with the attempt to find the bullion, even though the Indian danger was tenfold now that the remainder of the caravan was fleeing back across the Jornada.

"While the others were worrying about their scalps and thinking about how to get out of the country in a hurry, she was stocking this wagon with guns and grub and ammunition to make sure we'd have a fighting chance if we ran into trouble," he told Capehart.

Capehart barked, "Hi-yah!" and the wagon swung into motion.

The northbound wagons dwindled to tiny specks on the swells far astern of them. Soon these, and even the tiny banner of dust beneath which they marched, were lost over the rim of the hot horizon.

With Alex often traveling ahead on foot to scout their path, they veered away from the wheel ruts that marked the route to Santa Fe, and headed for broken country.

Following the run of the swales and avoiding all sky lines, they worked their way south and eastward until the main trail was at least ten miles to their right. For it was certain that if Indian war parties were still in the mood for taking scalps they would be watching the trail.

This added to the distance and made the going arduous. Both men and horses had been without water since the previous night. By midafternoon the animals were suffering. Alex could see Capehart, who was walking now to spare the wheel horse, moving with a mechanical, forced motion. Alex kept thinking of a big, cool spring that he had known as a boy near his birthplace in Missouri. At times, as he trudged exhaustedly along in the lengthening shadow of the wagon, he was seeing Char Shannon's dark eyes staring up at him from the depths of those crystal waters. Her eyes held that shining gladness he had seen when he had confided in her the vital clew to the trail of the treasure.

Then he would remember the fervor of the kiss which she had given Capehart. Always this would snap him back to the harsh reality of the sterile plains which imprisoned them, and of the pitiless sun that beat down on them—of jaded horses dragging a lurching wagon over sagebrush and rock. On every hand were alien bluffs and flat-topped hills and barren ridges baking in the sun—from which death, in buckskin and feathers, might swoop.

But the land seemed devoid of life. Great white clouds reared above the western horizon at midafternoon, intruding into a steel-blue sky, but that was the only change in the face of nature since morning.

Even these clouds came no nearer to give relief from the sun.

It was nearly sundown when the failing horses and failing men stumbled down to the course of the Cimarron, that strange and lonely river that came off the plains. The deadly Jornada was behind them. But it must be crossed again if they were to live.

18 ★ THE POINT where they reached the Cimarron was some distance below the lower springs. It was an unlovely spot, dry and desolate, with a forlorn stand of cottonwood and straggling willows forming a line along the flat, wandering, sandy river bed.

It was an upside-down stream, flowing mainly below the treacherous surface of the sand at this arid season of the year. Its sun-dried face was a trap, covering quicksands that could engulf a wagon and a team.

Pools of water showed here and there in the sandy channel, and Alex and Capehart were forced to double-hobble the pathetically eager horses to prevent a stampede into the quicksand.

They got out the wagon shovels and dug a pit near solid ground, which quickly filled with water. It was tinged with alkali and gritty with sand, but it was drinkable and it meant life to them all.

Revived, men and horses pushed downstream for a mile or more, with Alex leading the way and peering anxiously ahead, picking out landmarks.

Finally he broke into a run. He halted on the rim of a shallow barranca. Capehart joined him, and they stood gazing.

The remains of a burned prairie freight wagon lay in this dry gully. The bed of the vehicle had burned away, and the wheels were collapsing on half-consumed spokes.

Descending from the cutbank and walking near, they now saw grimmer relics in the debris—charred remains of men.

This was the spot to which Alex's wagons had been driven after the ambush. This was where the treasure had been placed in one wagon and this other vehicle and the bodies had been burned.

This was where Alex, wounded, half dead, had escaped that fate. It was from this point that the killers had started their own trip to death with the other wagon and the bullion.

Alex and Capehart buried the charred bones in a shallow grave and marked the spot with the burned wheels and iron tires from the destroyed wagon.

They scouted the vicinity. Alex found what they were seeking. He had not gone far downstream when he came upon wagon tracks in a stretch of soil that had been damp at that time but had dried to chalk hardness since.

He called Capehart. "That was my one hope," he said. "There were thunderstorms through this country at the time they got my wagons. I doubt if it has rained much since. That wagon was heavily loaded."

They traced the dried wheel tracks for another mile. Then twilight forced them to camp.

"They intended to follow the Cimarron east and cross to the Arkansas, so as to ford it below Fort Dodge," Alex said. "They didn't want to be seen at the fort, driving a Briscoe & Company wagon. They likely intended to cache the bullion somewhere along the way, once they got within reach of the settlements, and get rid of the wagon. Then they could have picked up the bullion again whenever the sign was right."

They made their camp in another of the dry barrancas near the river where a low cutbank offered cover for the small fire that they risked for the sake of hot food and coffee.

They picketed the horses on graze on an open flat beyond the rim of the gully. They were finishing their meal when Alex suddenly snatched up his rifle. Capehart had moved just as quickly in seizing up his Henry.

They backed away from the tiny glow of the fire, and the bitter thought was in Alex's mind that they had probably sold their lives for the sake of that warm meal.

There was movement in the dusty brush in the arroyo bottom. Then a girl's apprehensive voice called, "It's—it's me —Char! Are you there?"

Alex lowered his rifle. "Damnation!" he croaked.

"Hell's fire a'mighty!" Capehart said helplessly.

"It's them all right." Char's voice spoke happily. "I recognize them by their cussing. I told you I smelled coffee, Zack. I hope there's some water in this river we've been trying to find all day. I could soak in it for hours. And what I'd give for a nice big glass of cold beer right now."

She rode out of the brush into the firelight, followed by the lean, buckskin-shirted figure of Zack Dixon. Both of their horses were foot-heavy with weariness.

Alex and Capehart came striding angrily to meet them. Zack gave them a hangdog look. "I wanted to come alone," he said apologetically. "But she wouldn't have it. She kept a-sayin' thet with two of us the chances were twice as good that at least one would get through to find you. Tried to shake her off, but she's too danged bullheaded. An' so here she is."

"Keep your boiler pressure down, you two," Char sniffed. "It isn't Zack's fault. Anyway, it's done and can't be undone. If either of you had the instincts of human beings you'd help me off this poor beast. My legs seem to be paralyzed."

She wrinkled her nose at them in a way that Alex was beginning to find diverting. "Limbs to you, of course," she went on. "I remember now that you are the pair who think I dress like a strumpet. I'm sorry I'm not clad properly in skirts. They just didn't seem quite the thing for this sociable call."

She made a feeble attempt to dismount and failed. Alex lifted her from the saddle.

"Is that food I smell?" she said. "Bacon! Biscuits! And that wonderful coffee!"

He steadied her until circulation returned to her saddle-numbed legs. Zack Dixon was in little better shape. He walked woodenly, groaning with each step. "A fast ride," he said. "An' long."

"Which of you two rattleheads thought up this idea of following us?" Alex thundered.

"Let's not start calling names," Char remonstrated. "I might say things that would get my mouth washed out with soap."

"Zack, didn't you have sense enough to——?"

"Zack was the only one who tried to stop me," she said. "Nobody else would have cared. It was easy enough to pick up the trail of your wagon. In addition to that you had told me where to look."

"You haven't told us why you came," Alex snapped.

"I have my reasons," she said.

"We'll head back at midnight," Alex decided. "The stock will have had some rest by that time. We can make a dozen miles before daybreak, then hole up until dark again."

"Without the bullion?" she cried incredulously. "You wouldn't give up now when you're so near?"

"You know what would happen to you if you were captured down here," Alex said.

"Yes," she said hotly. "And do you know what would happen if you quit now and went back to Hays City? Morg Webb probably would give you a job swamping on some of his freight wagons, or maybe currying his saddle horses."

"Are you finished?" Alex said.

"Or is it Amelia Thayer you want to go back to?" she burst out. She was fighting back tears. She swung on her heels and walked away from him.

Alex caught her by the arm and swung her around to face him. "Why did you bring Amelia into this?" he demanded. "What have you learned?"

Char fought to escape from his grasp, but Alex kept his fingers locked about her wrists. Zack Dixon and Capehart stood watching, making no move to interfere.

She clamped her lips, and her eyes were dark and flat, barring him from any hint of her thoughts.

Suddenly his hands fell away from her. "Amelia planted Bill Stoker's watch on Len, didn't she?" he said. "You have believed that since the night it happened. Well, I was almost sure of it also. It was obvious."

He looked around at them. "I know why you kept quiet. You weren't sure where I stood."

"Amelia," Char said, "is a very magnetic person, and very well supplied with physical attractions. You would not have been the first man to be blinded by such charms."

118

Alex shrugged. "What puzzles me is how she came into possession of Bill's watch."

"Bart Grassman left his saddlebag in Morgan Webb's office when he first arrived in town that night. The watch must have been in it," Char said.

"How did you learn that?"

"From a dying man. His name was Pete Jackson. He was a swamper on one of Webb's wagons, and was hit by an arrow during the Indian fight. I took care of him, and he was very grateful. He died this morning, not long after you two had pulled out. But he told me many interesting things before the end came."

"Go on," Alex said.

"Pete Jackson believed your gun fight with Grassman was tied in with a lot of other rather odd events. He didn't particularly care for Morg Webb, even though he had worked for him for some time. He said he had been drinking that afternoon, and had crawled into the haymow in Webb's barn, where the saddle horses were stalled, to sleep it off. He was awakened not long after dark when he heard Grassman ride in and ask the night hostler where he could find Webb. Grassman mentioned that he'd been a week hiding out on the Jornada from the Indians. That explains why he reached Hays after you arrived.

"The hostler said Webb had left for my house. Grassman locked his horse in a stall and dropped the saddlebag in Webb's office, then hurried away on foot. Jackson heard the shooting and learned afterwards that you and Grassman had been in a gun fight. Later he heard Webb warn the hostler not to mention Grassman's visit to the wagon yards."

She paused a moment. "And before he died Pete Jackson told us something else that should clear up a lot of things. Morgan Webb was in Santa Fe at the time you were dickering for that treasure shipment."

"In Santa Fe!" Alex exclaimed.

Capehart came to his feet, spilling biscuits from the dutch oven. He and Alex stared at each other, their thoughts racing over past events, comprehension dawning upon them.

"Jackson said Webb made a fast trip to Santa Fe, arriving after you had pulled in with the spring caravan," Char said. "My guess is that he had got wind of that treasure shipment and wanted it for Overland Transport. Mail was still coming through at that time, you know. Jackson saw Webb and Bart Grassman powwowing in the corrals after dark. He guessed something was up, because Grassman was a mere bull-whacker who worked for my father's company. Webb kept out of sight in Santa Fe. And he left on the quiet. Jackson thinks he rode back to Hays alone."

Bleak acceptance formed in Alex. All the disconnected events had now moved into a complete pattern—an ugly pattern. And not only Morg Webb stood at the center of that pattern, but also Amelia. If she had planted the watch on Capehart, then she surely had knowledge of murder and ambush and robbery, and had attempted not only to aid the guilty person, but had tried to pin the crime on an innocent man.

"It's clear now why Bart Grassman was there at the gate of your house that night," he said. "He had just hit town and was anxious to tell Webb what had happened to the bullion. He probably stopped at Webb's wagon yard and learned that Morg had just left for your house to drive you to the Redfield party. I was the last person he expected to see. He believed he had left me for dead beyond the Jornada. He must have thought I was Webb when I came out of the house and walked down the path against the light. When he recognized me, his reaction was only natural. He went for his gun."

He was silent for a time. He was recalling how Ellis Thayer had turned to drinking, and the haunted look in the man's face. This also explained itself. Webb had persuaded Ellis to trick Char Shannon by selling to her a partnership that would ruin her company. Ellis had profited financially. Then he realized that murder was involved, and that more killings were in the making.

He reviewed the manner in which Ellis had died. Looking at the others, he surmised that their thoughts were running along the same line.

"Ellis Thayer was killed to keep him quiet," he said. "Webb did that."

"And it was Webb who sent that note to Jared Redfield, warning him that I faced financial trouble," Char exclaimed.

"Of course," Capehart joined in. "Of course it was. And it must have been Webb who tried to shoot you that night, Char. Now that I think back I don't recall seein' him in the car at the time the fireworks went off. It never occurred to me till now that he could have been the one."

"I doubt if he fired at Char," Alex said. "My guess is that it was Redfield he was after."

"Redfield!" Char exclaimed. "But why?"

"Because Redfield had just shown that he favored us on the grading contract and meant to give us every reasonable chance to make good. It would have been a mistake to have shot Redfield, maybe, but Morg was in no frame of mind to care. He was in the mood to kill at that moment. And tried to."

Char's voice tightened. "I don't believe there's any doubt as to who set fire to Dad's wagon yards last spring. Webb was in Hays at the time. That seems to have been the real start of his plan to take over the freighting business."

Capehart spoke. "Your paw's death likely was somethin' he hadn't counted on as a result of the fire. When he saw how easy it was to profit from such things he began to like the taste of blood. That's how all murderers start. It grows on 'em. It was only a step at a time for Morg to plan the ambush of Alex's wagons an' shoot at Jared Redfield. Ellis Thayer was the next to get in his way. An' now we're blockin' his path."

Alex looked at Char. "I apologize for calling you and Zack rattleheads," he said. "We're in your debt for turning back."

"There was nothing else to do," she said. "You had to be warned. Morg and his men will be waiting to ambush you somewhere up the trail when you and Len show up with the bullion. At the Arkansas River, probably. That must be why they headed north before the rest of the string turned back. They wanted a chance to drop out of sight."

Alex looked around. "We've made enough commotion here," he said. "We might have Indian visitors by daybreak. We'll rest a couple of hours after moonrise, then hit the trail."

They doused the fire as soon as Char and Zack had eaten. They picketed the two saddle horses on graze with the harness stock on the flat beyond the rim of the riverbank.

Char crawled tiredly into the wagon. Alex stood the first watch while Capehart and Zack slept, wrapped in blankets alongside the wagon.

He moved some distance away and chose a position where he could peer over the rim of the cutbank. The seven picketed horses were vague shapes on the flat, the sound of their grazing riding peacefully through the darkness.

The night was still and he could hear distant sounds—the single, unrepeated call of a lobo wolf, the cry of a night bird. On one occasion something aroused the coyotes, and their shrill yapping passed from one to another off into the depths of the plains.

121

Violent snorting and floundering arose from the river. Presently a band of elk emerged from the stream and passed within a few rods of him. They picked up either his scent or that of the horses and broke into pounding flight.

The nocturnal wind of the plains sprang up with its customary abruptness, sharp and chill. It rattled through the brush, and this covered all other sounds. The waning moon rose in a sky swept clear of all clouds and gave light enough so that the wagon and the sleeping forms of Capehart and Zack Dixon were distinct against the white sand of the dry river bed.

After another hour Alex aroused Capehart. "Turn us all out a couple of hours after midnight," he said.

He rolled up in a blanket alongside Zack. But sleep would not come at once. He kept thinking of Morgan Webb, and of Amelia. The cold horror deepened within him.

The wind flapped the wagon sheets. He heard Char cry out in her sleep. She uttered Capehart's name. Then his. She was dreaming over again that terrible moment of the hand-to-hand struggle during the Indian attack.

Without warning, rifle flame spurted from two points on the rim of the cutbank fifty yards away. A bullet broke a spoke in a wheel inches from Alex's head.

He plunged from his blankets and scrambled for his rifle, which he had stood against the wheel. Zack, shouting something, was rearing from his sleep also.

More bullets were seeking them, their whining passage as savage as the snarl of wild dogs. Two rifles were firing. Out in the flats Alex heard more guns in action.

The solid, driving impact of a bullet in flesh came. Zack Dixon uttered a choked, sighing sound. He tried to say Alex's name. He failed and pitched forward on his face.

Alex had found his Henry rifle. He fired one shot before a crushing weight struck him down. Searing pain engulfed him. Blackness came.

Out in the flats a wounded horse screamed. That was broken off as more bullets struck home.

At last the guns quit.

Capehart, who had been on watch a distance up the wash, came working his way from cover to cover through the moonlight, his face predatory. He crawled to the rim of the cutbank, but seemed to find no target for he did not fire. The booming wind, which had covered the approach of their assailants, now smothered the sounds of their departure.

Char slid from the wagon, half clad. Capehart called to her, "Stay there."

He went moving out into the flat on foot. Char wheeled and looked down at the two sprawled figures at her feet.

She said numbly, "Alex! Zack!"

Her voice rose to a scream. "ALEX!"

19 ★ AS FROM a far distance Alex heard Capehart's voice say, "He's comin' out of it at last."

Presently he was gazing again into that crystal-cold spring of his boyhood, and once more it was Char Shannon's eyes that he was seeing in the depths of that azure water. Her gaze was desperately urgent, as though insisting on something.

He found himself trying to respond—trying to do this thing —whatever it was—just to please her, and to end that great anxiety that gripped her.

Then there was no cool spring. But Char's eyes were still before him, and very real, looking down at him. Her face was pale and drawn.

Capehart was present too, gazing with that same demand. Gradually he became aware that he lay in a tiny pocket amid a thicket of willows. The sun was beating down.

Char's face came nearer. "Alex!" Her voice held that fierce appeal he had seen in her eyes. "Alex! You are back with us. You are alive! You are going to live if you try! You must try!"

He knew then the importance of her message. Painfully he forced his will to meet that request. All his shocked nerves wanted to quit. Only his mind recognized the danger and fought against it.

Slowly the numbness was driven back. Soon he became aware that he was stripped naked and lying beneath a blanket. He drifted away into blackness once more. There were times when he again heard Char calling his name and demanding that he answer. Finally he began to try. At last he was able to reply. But that seemed to take a long time and great effort.

Abruptly he came completely out of the coma. His head was clear. His eyes opened and remained open. He said, "I'm back. I kept hearing you call me, Char."

She was bending over him with the look of a person whose prayers have been answered. "You—you're going to live!" she breathed. Then she wept without restraint.

Alex strengthened. Capehart rolled a smoke and placed it between his lips. "A bullet clipped you across the back of the neck," he explained. "It grazed a vertebra, an' we were afraid it might have hit the spinal cord. But if it had, you wouldn't be perkin' up. Even so, you kept sinkin' down. Char wouldn't stand for it. She forced breath into your lungs from her own lips. She kept you warm with her own body."

"I remember that rifles opened up on us," Alex said. He aroused, lifted his head, and looked at them searchingly. "What about Zack Dixon? He was hit!"

Capehart made a helpless gesture. "Done for. I buried him as best I could."

A long silence held. "Was it Indians?" Alex finally asked.

"No."

"Morgan Webb?"

"Who else?" Capehart said. "They rode shod horses. There were four or more of 'em. I found their trail yesterday. They had a wagon waitin' for 'em a couple of miles away."

"Yesterday!" Alex exclaimed. He looked incredulously at the sun. "Did you say—yesterday?"

"You've been out more than a full day," Capehart explained. "You opened your eyes for a few minutes yesterday, then went under again. This is the second day since they jumped us."

Alex sat up abruptly. "We've got to—to——!" he began. Their faces began spinning before his eyes, and he sagged back.

"Take it easy!" Capehart said. "We should have guessed they'd do exactly what they did. We took it for granted they were headin' for the Arkansas to wait for us to show up there. We ought to have known Morg Webb wouldn't run away from one hundred an' fifty thousand dollars, even at the risk of his scalp. He figured you'd come back alive from the buffalo stampede. It was only a blind when he pulled out, headin' north with Keno Dane an' his roughs.

"They circled back, cut our trail, and followed it till they came to the ashes of the first wagon. That was all they needed to know. They didn't have to let you live any longer. Nor me. They didn't want any witnesses to show up later. So, after they had located our camp, they hung back until the wind came up an' the moon rose to give light, then moved in. What they didn't know was that Char and Zack had pulled

124

in. They mistook Zack for me when they opened up. They think they got both of us, or at least left us with some holes in us that'll prevent us from ever gettin' out of this country alive. They didn't believe it was worth while to move in closer to make sure. Or didn't want to pick up any hot lead themselves, if one or the other of us was still able to use a gun."

Alex again tried to get to his feet. "They've found the bullion by this time," he said thickly. "Where's our wagon and horses? We've got to . . . !"

His voice faded off. Capehart nodded. "We left the wagon back there in the river bottom, where they jumped us," he said. "It wasn't of any use to us anyway. They slaughtered the horses. Every last one of 'em."

Alex remained propped on an elbow, staring. For the second time he was afoot and wounded, with the desolate Jornada between him and the settlements. This time his situation was shared by two more humans. And there was in him the dread that he might be a fatal handicap to their survival.

He sagged back on the blankets. Char remained at his side while Capehart moved off through the brush to stand watch.

She correctly guessed the depth of his bitterness. "You can't blame yourself," she said. "We all should have seen these things. We should have known Webb would trail you."

"I'll get you out of this," he said. "You, above all. You don't deserve to die in this desert."

She sat looking at him, a softness in her eyes. She smiled a little. Presently Alex slept—soundly.

Death had missed him by a narrow margin, but the last of the numbing nerve shock was fading. By morning the following day he was insisting that he was able to travel. By afternoon even Char conceded that he could make the attempt. She surrendered to him his clothes, which he had been demanding.

"At least I've got a gun or two this time," he said. "I was barehanded the last time I walked the Jornada."

"We've likely got another advantage," Capehart said. "They think we're dead, or too used up to travel. The point is that Webb won't move any faster than necessary. He's got to take it slow an' careful, especially in daytime, or some Indian hunting party will spot him. That might give us a chance to catch up with him. But if he suspects we're on his trail he'll likely run like a scorched cat."

They set out after the heat of late afternoon began to ease a trifle. Alex and Capehart carried food packs. They had the two canteens that had been among the wagon's equipment. Water would not be a problem for the present, for they were following the trail of Webb's wagon along the river, but the canteens would be vital once they turned north into the Jornada.

Capehart led the way, followed by Char. She tried to match his long stride, but was forced to settle for moving along at a half trot. She was hard-pressed but did not utter a complaint. It was Alex who called to Capehart to slow the march.

After they had hiked for two hours through sand and sun-baked flats, the trail brought them back to the river, where there was an open pool. Char raced ahead to kneel and drink thirstily.

"Delicious!" she sighed rapturously. "Absolutely exquisite! Even the gritty part."

She had laid aside her hat. Her hair hung in two braids down her back. She lifted water in her hands, poured it down the back of her neck. She giggled like a child.

Alex moved suddenly, picked her up in his arms, kissed her. He sat her down and said in a strained voice, "All right. I've wanted to do this ever since that day in Santa Fe a long time ago."

He seized up his rifle and pack again and walked onward. Without saying a word Char slung her blanket roll over her shoulder and went hurrying after him and dropped into step close at his heels.

The fresh tracks of Webb's wagon followed the weathered traces left by the treasure-laden vehicle Grassman and his men had driven down the Cimarron more than a month in the past.

At times the faint trail had been eroded away for long stretches, and then Webb's men had circled on horseback until they had been sure they were still on the route. These delays had cost Webb hours of time, and were to the advantage of the three who trailed him on foot.

Darkness drove them into camp at last, darkness and Alex's weariness, for he had been a trifle optimistic of his swift recuperation.

However, at daybreak he was fit and ready, and they resumed the dogged, step-by-step journey, with those fresh wagon tracks paralleling the old marks of the treasure wagon.

At one point Alex plucked from brush a long strand of fine brown hair. He looked at the others. Amelia was still with Morgan Webb. He had feared this would be so. In
126

fact, she would have had no alternative. But he was sure Amelia had other reasons also.

He let the strand blow away in the hot noon breeze, and they walked on.

It was toward sundown of the third day, and Alex knew they were near the lower spring of the Cimarron—a route not used for years by freighters—when he sighted the charred running gear of the treasure wagon ahead.

They all broke from their weariness and began running. The coyote-scattered bones of several humans lay about. These were the relics of Grassman's companions who had died at the hands of Indians.

Fresh boot tracks had trodden down the loose, hot soil over a wide area. This was the evidence of the feverish search Webb and his men had made for the bullion cache.

And they had found it! The signs were all plain enough!

Grassman's men had made their final stand in the shelter of a sandy cutbank in a shallow dry creek bed not fifty yards from the burned wagon.

It was here they saw evidence of the excavation of a shallow cache. It was evident that Grassman's men had buried the bullion boxes in the sandy soil just beneath this cutbank, and that the Indians had not suspected the presence of the treasure only a few inches beneath the bodies of the defenders who had been slain there.

Webb's wagon had been driven to this spot. Alex stopped and picked up a loose object. It was a Mexican hidalgo, a coin, which had been tramped into the sand beneath a boot. "There was a bag of 'em," he said. "A leather bag. It must have busted open."

He pocketed it and added wryly, "Well, we got some of the treasure back."

"Webb's wagon was riding light when it came to this spot and heavy when it left," Capehart said. "They got the bullion, no doubt about it."

"They're less than twenty-four hours ahead of us," Alex said. "They can't travel any faster than we can with that wagon through tough country—if we keep going."

20 ★ AT TWILIGHT the next day they headed into the Jornada, with the North Star as their guide. The thin moon was up, and their pallid shadows marched with them. By midnight Alex judged they were nearly a dozen miles along the fifty-mile route of the Jornada. There was no way of knowing exact distances. Except for Webb's wagon, whose tracks they were not attempting to trace out in the darkness, no wheelmark had ever been made on this plain.

The main route to Santa Fe was at least forty miles west of them, and even that path likely would see no more travel until spring came again with its new promise of peace and hope.

"It's my guess Webb will use the lower trail, but will leave it this side of the Arkansas and cross below Fort Dodge," Alex said. "He wouldn't want to be seen at the fort with a heavy load in a wagon that was riding light when they deserted the string."

The chill midnight wind of the plains sprang up. Alex could see Char cringing, and huddling deeper into the collar of her saddle jacket.

She stumbled and said, "My feet are all thumbs."

A coyote lifted its greeting far away, and she shuddered.

Capehart said soothingly, "By tomorrow night we should be at the Arkansas. Then that old moon-dog will sing another tune."

Alex called a halt at intervals. Each time, they would press together for the sake of warmth in the lee of some rock or hummock.

Dawn arrived. They kept going until the sun came up. Then they discovered that buffalo were drifting across their route ahead. They decided it was the same herd that Alex and Len had stampeded to save the wagon train.

Here and there, far in the distance, the saffron glint of dust rose in the vicinity of the buffalo. Alex and Capehart looked at each other. There was no question about what was causing those dust spurts. Indian hunting parties were working along the fringe of the herd.

"We'll have to hole up," Alex said. "I'd hoped it might be safe to push on until the sun was well up. It looks like we'll have to hide out until dark."

Weary, disappointed, they found cover at the base of an eroded clay bluff and camped. They knew this delay ended any chance they might have had of overtaking Webb this side of the Arkansas.

They discovered the recent tracks of wagons and riders near the bluff. The traces were less than a day old. Webb had passed this way with his gunmen and the laden wagon. The marks indicated they had paused for some hours, and had then pushed on toward the Arkansas.

"They got through ahead of the buffalo," Alex said. "Looks like they're traveling at night mainly too, and holing up during the day."

He looked at the others. "Let's hope they made it through. We know now for sure they're aiming to by-pass Fort Dodge. That means they're heading direct for Hays. Our best bet now is to walk straight for the fort and get horses. Maybe we can overtake 'em before they reach Hays. Fort Dodge should be directly north of us—the shortest distance across the Jornada from here."

"Let's hope the buffalo have moved out of our way by dark, or it might be a pretty far piece," Capehart said.

They ate cold biscuits and cold smoked buffalo tongue and drank a ration of water from the canteens.

Alex stood the first watch while the others slept. He moved to a vantage point where he could watch the plains. Both the buffalo and the dust spurts were nearer and moving in a southwesterly direction across the plains some five or six miles away. He could see the Indian spearmen killing shaggy beasts.

His glance kept turning to Char Shannon. She lay sleeping, a hand lying on Capehart's arm in an attitude of deep affection.

The great buffalo herd continued to flow over the eastern horizon until all the plains north of them became a spotted carpet of black and buff.

Presently a new streamer of dust formed to the east. Beneath that a big Indian village on the move emerged. They were Comanches, and they passed by only a mile away. Alex saw warriors who were riding in advance pull up, staring at the ground. There was a boil of excitement and long, chattering palaver and much pointing.

Finally the Indians rode on. They had found the tracks of the wagon, but evidently had decided to stay with the meat hunting rather than try to overtake a quarry that had more than a day's lead.

Thus did Morgan Webb's luck continue to hold.

The Comanches vanished to the southwest, heading for water at the Cimarron, no doubt. All other signs of Indians also faded during the afternoon. But there seemed no end to the buffalo herd. By sundown the route to the Arkansas appeared to be blocked as far as the eye could carry to the east and west.

"We can't wait until that herd passes," Alex said. "It might be another day or two. We're already down to our last swallow of water. If we can't hit for the Arkansas tonight we'll have to go back to the Cimarron."

"We'll go through the herd." Char spoke.

"If they started runnin', we'd be squashed like you'd stomp on a tumblebug," Capehart said.

"What would we do back at the Cimarron?" she argued. "Wait until some Indians came along to finish us off? We must go north if we ever expect to catch up with Webb before he disposes of that bullion. The buffalo didn't stampede the night you and Alex walked through them."

Alex and Capehart looked at each other. Alex finally shrugged. "There's no other way," he said. "Maybe we'll make it, maybe not."

At sunset they shouldered their packs and left the concealment of the bluff. The sinking sun cast long shadows. Alex eyed his companions.

Capehart was a wild, unshaven figure as he strode along, his worn hat jammed low over his long, thin face, his alkali-stained breeches cuffed high above his boots. He had his rifle and six-shooters slung on his back, along with the food pack, for better balance, as had Alex.

Char was wind-burned. Alkali powdered her eyelashes and hair. Her eyes seemed larger and very dark. She was tired, but she possessed reservoirs of endurance, for she moved along proudly with her lithe stride as though resolved to conquer all hardships and privation. She even had the audacity to swing her hips provocatively when she became aware she was under Alex's observation. "It keeps their minds off their troubles," she said in an off-stage whisper.

Capehart shook his head resignedly. "Ain't she somethin'," he said.

Darkness came before they reached the outer fringe of the buffalo herd. The shaggy, ungainly, high-shouldered beasts loomed before them in the starlight.

Char moved closer to Alex. Her hand clung to his, and he could feel the tension throbbing in her.

They walked deeper into the herd. Around them the darkness was alive with the stir and snuffling and grunting of the animals. The buffalo were still grazing steadily southwestward toward the Cimarron. As was their nature, they traveled

130

in loose formation and in bands that were separated from the others sometimes by hundreds of yards.

But there was a cohesion also in this mighty assembly. These beasts answered to a mass instinct that was unpredictable.

At times an animal would take fright at the appearance of the three figures in the starlight, and would go lumbering away, causing an uneasy commotion. Once a score or more of animals began running, and the humans halted, frozen and quailing. But again the herd quieted around them. And again they breathed. Presently they dared resume their nerve-strung journey.

There was no halting for rest. Midnight came. A dying moon was a slash of silver in the sky. Its glow revealed clearly the deadly possibilities of their situation.

Alex was beginning to imagine buffalo where there were no buffalo. Then again he would almost walk into animals without seeing them until the last moment.

Char's stride lost its drive. She was stumbling often. He had his arm around her, helping her.

At last he began to realize that there really were no buffalo. The clumsy shapes around which they had walked with such taut care for hours were no longer there in the moonlight. The snorting and the snuffling were behind them.

"We're clear!" he croaked. "We're through the herd."

They rested until the strain of those hours had faded out of their nerves. Then they moved on. They were unutterably weary now, lifting one foot after the other. At times Alex and Capehart carried Char along almost bodily. Afterwards they would sink down again until they could force themselves to rise and move on.

Daybreak! They stared from bloodshot eyes. They might as well have been back at the bluff from which they had started the journey through the buffalo herd the previous night. They faced nothing but the changeless plains—the same types of swells and sear yellow bluffs and dry washes that were as gray white as picked bones.

There was no sign of the Arkansas. They slept a few hours, then moved ahead again. They risked the chance of being sighted by Indians by traveling in daylight, for they felt that death was inevitable anyway unless they reached the river soon.

The canteens had been empty since the previous night. Alex's tongue was swollen. At times he was positive he glimpsed Indians riding toward them. But when he would halt, lifting his rifle, there would be only the hot, vacant land staring impersonally at him.

They kept stumbling ahead. The thought came to Alex that this was all life held in store for them now—mechanical motion until they dropped and died in the glare of the blazing sun.

Sundown came. Char fell, and Alex tried to lift her, but only staggered a step, and both of them went down.

Then deep and far came a sullen, solid impact that hit the ears with its weight.

Capehart's head lifted. "Cannon!" he croaked. "The sunset gun at Fort Dodge! We're there!"

Inspired, they arose and broke into a staggering run. They came over a rise that had stubbornly hidden this sight from them—and in the distance beyond the river made out the smoke of evening fires and the flat shape of the stockade at Fort Dodge.

They stumbled down that long slope, fought their way through sand to the river. Life strengthened in them as they drank the alkali-tinged water. Presently they sighted a patrol from the post on the south shore. Alex fired a signal shot. Soon ambulances and outriders came splashing across a ford to pick them up.

Peering through the twilight as they neared the fort, Alex saw wagons with bare hoops and smoke-blackened cargoes camped outside the stockade. It was their own battle-grimed caravan which had arrived back at the army post.

Men came hurrying to meet them as they alighted at the wagon camp. Among them was one of Alex's drivers, Jed Carey. He stared as he would at ghosts. "What in tophet happened to——?" he began.

"Jed, have you seen anything of Morg Webb and his outfit?" Alex demanded.

"Webb? Why, a scoutin' detail reported passin' Webb's wagon on the trail not fur north o' here about noon today. They must have forded the Arkansas east o' here. They was headin' fer the Pawnee Fork on their way back to Hays. They must have got hung up somewhere on the Jornada. By rights, they should have been in Hays long ago."

"Amelia Thayer?" Alex asked.

"She was still with 'em." Jed answered. "I talked with one o' the troopers who was with the patrol."

Alex and Capehart looked at each other. "Webb's in reach!" Alex breathed thankfully. "The Lord is kind to us.

We can still catch up before he makes it to Hays if we have luck."

He whirled on Jed Carey. "We need two saddle horses. Good ones."

"Make it three!" Char spoke.

Jed peered, astonished. "None o' you look like yo're in shape fer a hundred-mile ride," he said. "But if yo're in such an all-fired hurry to raise some mounts there're buffalo hunters marooned here with plenty o' horseflesh on their hands. The trail's said to be safe north to the Pawnee Fork. All the Injuns seem to have pulled south o' the Arkansas to hunt buffalo."

Alex and Capehart and Char began hurrying toward the campfires of the buffalo hunters.

21 ★ ALEX SUDDENLY pulled up the tough-mouthed buffalo pony he was riding and made a warning gesture to Capehart and Char, who also were mounted on ewe-necked half-broken ponies.

It was sundown on the second day out of Fort Dodge. They had camped north of the Pawnee Fork the previous night, and now Hays City was over the sky line no more than five miles distant.

He and Capehart let their ponies drift ahead until they could peer over a swell. He said quietly, "There they are at last!"

All day they had been following the freshening tracks of the same heavily laden wheels that had pulled out of that dry wash beyond the Jornada where the treasure cache had been looted.

And now their quarry was in sight. Less than two miles ahead a prairie wagon, tiny at that distance, was moving along the trail toward the faint haze of smoke over the prairie that marked the location of Hays City.

Men rode as outriders. Alex could make out Morg Webb's cream-colored hat. And he saw the flutter of a woman's white dress in the wagon bow. Amelia.

He had feared that Webb might have cached the bullion somewhere along the trail to wait until he was positive he was not suspected, but the deep wheelmarks showed that the treasure was still in the wagon.

"Morg's sure of himself," he said to the others. "He thinks we're dead, and that he can freight the stuff right into town without anyone suspecting anything out of the ordinary."

Char joined them and stood in the stirrups, peering. She watched the creeping wagon, straining on tiptoe to see above the grassy crest of the rise. "They've timed it so they'll pull into Hays after dark," she said.

They moved ahead presently, staying far astern of the creeping wagon and below the sky line. When twilight deepened, they drew nearer their quarry.

Darkness had come when they passed Fort Hays, then forded Big Creek into sight of the town. The stream was still roiled from the passing of Webb's wagon.

Once again Alex watched the lights of Hays City brighten and stretch like a bright necklace across the dark prairie as he rode toward it. He thought of that other night when he had come out of the darkness of this same trail—back from the Jornada.

That had seemed long, long ago. It also seemed incongruous that Hays would be so unchanged, so complacent. For someone soon was likely to die, and Alex knew the chances were that it would be himself. He gazed at the same tents, the same outline of shacks and false fronts, the same glow of light over the saloon district—even heard the carnal laughter of a woman somewhere. It had not changed, but he had changed.

Capehart rode at his side in silence, and Alex knew they shared this dismal mood. Capehart, too, knew that this must be settled with guns.

And Char stayed close beside them, as though she were aware that this might be a time for parting forever, and that companionship was precious.

They crossed the K.P. tracks and rode through crooked lanes, past the shabby fringe town of tents and shacks. The dust of Webb's wagon hung in the air ahead of them, glinting golden in the beams of lamplight, so close were they at his heels.

Char spoke. "Get Hickok. He'll help you. It's his job." Her voice was thin and high.

"There's little time for hunting help," Alex said. "They won't waste minutes hiding that bullion."

Hoxie Carver's house loomed up, and he said, "Stay here until we come back."

Char leaped from the saddle and barred their path as they

134

dismounted. "Wait!" she said brokenly. "You can't go there —just the two of you. They are too many for you."

Alex took her in his arms and kissed her. "There's nothing I want more than to stay here with you," he said.

Her dark eyes were swimming. She said, "Len is like a brother to me. And you—you're more than that."

Alex and Capehart walked away, leaving her standing there, her hands at her bosom as though the icy hand of desolation had touched her.

They strode side by side down a dark street, then swung right. Directly before them lay Webb's wagon yards and barns and corrals, spreading widely into the shadows.

Webb had driven the treasure wagon into the tunnel of a big, hip-roofed barn which fronted on the street. The sliding door at the entrance was still open, and shadows were moving against the light of a lantern whose glow was strengthening as someone adjusted the wick.

They walked nearer, and now they saw saddle-stiffened men, dusty and irritable, stripping their gear from the jaded horses at the feed corral in the yards away from the barn. Webb's big, creamy-hued hat was among them.

They walked to the door of the wagon barn and peered cautiously. The wagon stood there, bulking black and misshapen against the light of the lantern which hung beyond. A hostler had just unhooked the horses, and now the animals moved out of the barn with a rush of hooves, heading for feed and rest in corrals that were home to them.

Amelia alighted from the wagon, clambering down over the high bow, then reached back and lifted down a small carpetbag and her reticule. She had no help in this.

Webb and Keno Dane entered the barn from the wagon yard, carrying their saddles, which they slung on racks in the adjoining tackroom.

"Horses always come first," Amelia said crossly. "I barked my ankle climbing out of that infernal wagon. Morgan, lift out my trunk like a nice man. We'll carry it into your office."

Keno Dane had a stone jug of whiskey in his hand. He tilted it with the greed of a man long denied his regular ration. One of his gunmen, a loose-coupled individual, appeared and stood eagerly waiting his turn.

Webb glared around and shouted angrily for the hostler. "I told you to shut and lock that damned outside door!" he raged.

The man hurried to obey. Alex and Capehart drew back as he approached to roll the sliding door and cut off view from the street.

Then Alex moved in, caught the hostler roughly by the shoulder. "It stays open," he murmured.

Capehart jammed a pistol muzzle in the man's stomach. Alex stepped into the barn. Webb and Amelia had their backs to him. Keno Dane and the gangling man were busy with the jug.

Alex moved to the wagon. Shielded from their view, he pulled himself over the rear bow and lowered himself silently into the interior. The light reached dimly here. He stood on a cargo covered by worn tarpaulins. Amelia's leather trunk was still in the wagon.

Drawing his knife, he slashed a tarp. Beneath it were heavy iron boxes, still padlocked. These contained the silver bullion and gold he had contracted to deliver at Hays. The treasure seemed to be intact.

He dropped to the ground. The leathery man, lowering the jug, sighted him.

The man stood frozen an instant. Then he screeched, "It's Alex Briscoe! Gawd!"

He dropped the jug and his hand flipped to his holster. He was a professional gunman and fast. But Alex beat him. The reports blended, but Alex's bullet had struck before his opponent's hammer touched off powder. The shock of it sent the other's shot wild.

Keno Dane whirled, then dove beneath a wagon which was hoisted on jacks for repairs in the yard. Dane's pistol roared twice from that shelter. A bullet tugged malevolently at Alex's sleeve. He fired back into the shadows—but without apparent result.

Morgan Webb had taken one great lunging stride out of the barn, lifting Amelia with him. He was in shadow also now, and from that position he opened up. But Alex had side-stepped to shelter back of the treasure wagon. Bullets raked the underside of the wagon, ricocheting from gear and tires around him, but he escaped unhurt.

He heard Webb and Amelia retreating at a run across the open wagon yard. Behind him Capehart fired two shots. Someone began groaning in the street. Evidently one or more of Dane's men had attempted to flank them from that direction.

Both Alex and Capehart were now driven into the wagon tunnel, where they were exposed to the lanternlight. Alex
136

turned his gun on the lantern, and his bullet shattered it, sending a burning shower from the wick. They were left in darkness. Alex smelled spilled kerosene amid the reek of gunpowder fumes.

"We got to get out of here before they get this place surrounded," he said. "This way."

They moved to the inner door, then raced into the wagon yard. Gunfire thundered from the shadows, but Dane and his men had not expected them to come in this direction. This was attack, not retreat, and it had taken them by surprise. Their fire was hurried and wild.

Crouching, they made twenty strides and reached the corral, where mules and horses were milling in terror. Alex jerked the gate bars, and the stock streamed past with a thunderous clatter of hooves. The wagon yard was filled with frenzied animals, milling about and rearing.

Alex guessed that Webb had headed for his office and living quarters. Covered by the confusion of the stampeding stock, he and Capehart raced to a side door of this structure.

It was locked. Alex blew the lock from the door with a bullet. He kicked the portal open.

Immediately a six-shooter began flaming in the dark room, the bullets sweeping through the opening. But Alex had moved aside.

He called, "Amelia!"

Her terror-filled voice responded, but he could not understand the words.

"Let her come out, Webb!" he shouted. "And come out yourself with your hands up, or I'll come in and get you."

Amelia began pleading frantically with Webb. The spat of a fist meeting flesh came, and her voice broke off.

Someone yelled, "The wagon barn's on fire!" Alex remembered the lantern he had smashed.

He said to Capehart, "I'm going in. Shoot over me into the ceiling through that door."

Crouching, he dashed into the room. The concussions of Capehart's gun at his back deafened him, and he could feel the heat of the powder flashes darting above him.

Then he was in the room. He fell headlong over a chair. The roar of Webb's gun overrode all other sound. But the fall had saved him, for Webb had shot high.

In the gunflash he glimpsed Webb. The man had taken refuge back of a sofa near the wall, and was standing, exposed only from the waist up, a revolver in each hand. Alex saw Amelia at the opposite end of the room, huddled on the floor.

He fired twice at Webb as darkness clapped down again. He went leaping through the blackness to come to hand-to-hand grips. He found his quarry—but what he found was a dead man.

Both of his bullets, fired in the dark, had torn through Morgan Webb's chest. Only the tight quarters into which Webb had wedged himself back of the sofa held him upright.

A red glow was working into the room through the windows. Flames were bursting through the roof of the barn. A fire bell was clanging in town.

Capehart came into the room, which was alight now with the red reflection.

"Webb is dead," Alex said. "Amelia's in here."

He holstered his own guns as he moved toward Amelia's huddled figure, and he saw Capehart do the same.

"Keno Dane's here too." Dane's bitter voice spoke behind them.

Dane's gun roared at the same instant, and Alex heard the bullet tear into Capehart's body.

Dane had entered through the office at the front and had shot Capehart in the back.

Alex pivoted and drew. Capehart, staggering under the blow of the bullet, also drew his right-hand gun and fired even as he was reeling.

This was the pattern of Len Capehart's life—the moment when the bullet in the back that he had always expected had cut him down. His return shot was the instinctive reaction of a man whose will had been trained to meet such a situation.

Dane fired a second time. This shot was intended for Alex. But it went wide. For Dane was dead almost before the bullet sped from the gun.

Death had struck him down from two sources. Both Alex and Capehart had registered dead center on their target. Their slugs had torn through Keno Dane's brain. His body was hurled back into the unlighted office, where it fell on the bare floor.

Morgan Webb still swayed in his grotesque position, his death-shocked eyes gazing unseeingly at the destruction of all his plans. Flames were leaping higher. More of his crew lay dead or wounded in the wagon yard. The remainder seemed to have given up the fight. The shooting had ended.

Then Webb went limp and fell out of sight. Amelia, who had not known until then that he had his death wound, screamed in terrible understanding, and fainted.

Alex said frantically, "Len! Len!"

Capehart reeled against a wall, tried to grip a window frame for support. He said, a deep regret in his eyes, "Tell . . . Tell—Char . . . !"

He could not finish it. Alex caught him as he pitched forward, and eased his body to the floor.

Alex kept saying, "Len! Len!" He couldn't stop.

Char came into the room, followed by Wild Bill Hickok. She rushed to Capehart's side and knelt. Her face was completely colorless. She buried her face in her hands and began to sob.

Alex said huskily, "Wait!"

Capehart had stirred. His eyes opened. He looked at Alex, a ghost of a smile on his pain-twisted lips. "Well, being a brother to her is next best, at least," he said. "You have all the luck, Briscoe."

"Fetch a doctor!" Wild Bill yelled. He bent over Capehart. "You're not going to cash in, Len," he went on. "It wouldn't be right."

Alex gazed at Char. Her eyes searched his questioningly for a moment, and then with soaring gladness as she saw an answer there. "I'm mighty glad you don't look on me as a brother," he said.

He lifted her to her feet. "Remember that day in Santa Fe?" he said. "You were a slip of a girl and I fell in love with you then. I wouldn't admit it."

She kissed him with a full and womanly richness. "How long and how happily I will always remember that day," she said, "—and also this day."

Afterwards he and Char stood in the Gem saloon, which had been converted into a hospital. Will Lewis, the doctor, worked on Capehart, who lay on a sheet-covered table. Another doctor attended one of Webb's gunmen.

Three blanket-wrapped bodies lay on stretchers in a corner. Webb and Keno Dane and the leathery-jawed man. Through the window Alex could see the fire. All of Webb's barns and wagons were burning, and the men of the town were fighting only to prevent the spread of the flames.

Amelia sat in a chair, her face waxen. She was wondering if Morgan Webb had carried out his threat to mail a letter from Fort Dodge which was to be opened in case of his death.

Hickok entered the room on tiptoe, looked at the sheeted forms, and removed his hat. "Hoxie Carver asked me to tell you, Alex, that they weren't able to get Webb's wagon out of the barn in time, like you asked him to try to do. It's burning, along with the rest of the outfit."

"No matter," Alex said. "Bullion won't burn. Nor gold coin. We'll dig it out of the ashes. Just see that it's guarded until we can get at it."

Amelia heard that. She came to her feet with an anguished scream. "My money!" she cried. "My twenty thousand dollars! The money Char Shannon paid my husband for his share of Briscoe & Company. It—it—merciful heavens! It was in my trunk in that wagon."

She whirled on Char in a frothing rage. "It was in bank notes. Paper money! And now it's gone too—and you have everything! Even Alex! And I have nothing!"

She advanced on Char, demonical fury in her. But Wild Bill seized her and carried her bodily out of the Gem. She was still kicking and screaming insanely.

Will Lewis straightened and stepped back from Capehart at last and said, "Len should make it now. The bullet missed the lung. His pulse is already beginning to respond. Men like him have great recuperative powers. They're——"

"Fighting men," Char said. "And one of them is going to be my husband." She kissed Alex with vast tenderness.